Acting Edition

Twelfth Night

A Musical Adaptation of
William Shakespeare's
Twelfth Night

Conceived by
Kwame Kwei-Armah
and Shaina Taub

Music and Lyrics by
Shaina Taub

I0591835

concord
theatricals

FOR PRODUCTION INQUIRIES

UNITED STATES AND CANADA
info@concordtheatricals.com
1-866-979-0447

UNITED KINGDOM AND EUROPE
licensing@concordtheatricals.co.uk
020-7054-7298

Each title is subject to availability from Concord Theatricals Corp.,
depending upon country of performance. Please be aware that
TWELFTH NIGHT may not be licensed by Concord Theatricals Corp.
in your territory. Professional and amateur producers should contact
the nearest Concord Theatricals Corp. office or licensing partner to
verify availability.

THIRD-PARTY MATERIALS USE NOTE

IMPORTANT BILLING AND CREDIT REQUIREMENTS

TWELFTH NIGHT was originally commissioned and produced by The Public Theater (Oskar Eustis, Artistic Director; Patrick Willingham, Executive Director) and premiered at the Delacorte Theater in Central Park, New York, on September 2, 2016. The performance was directed by Kwame Kwei-Armah, with music direction by Shaina Taub, sets by David Zinn, costumes by Andrea Hood, lights by Amith Chandrashaker, choreography by Lorin Latarro, and orchestrations by Mike Brun. The Production Stage Manager was Evangeline Rose Whitlock. The cast was as follows:

VIOLA . . . . Nikki M. James

COUNTESS OLIVIA . . . . .Nanya-Akuki Goodrich

DUKE ORSINO . . . . .Jose Llana

FESTE . . . . Shaina Taub

MALVOLIO . . . . Andrew Kober

SIR TOBY BELCH . . . . .Jacob Ming-Trent

MARIA . . . . Lori Brown-Niang

SIR ANDREW . . . . Daniel Hall

SEBASTIAN . . . . .Troy Burton

ANTONIO . . . . David Weaver, Sr.

FABIAN . . . . Patrick J. O'Hare

ORSINO'S ATTENDANT . . . . Benjamin Levine

OLIVIA'S ATTENDANT . . . . Elvis Reyes

OFFICERS . . . . .Eddie Bottoms, Ella Evans

WEDDING SINGER . . . . .Vivian Jett

MARIA'S MESSENGER . . . . Lorenzo Hudson

ILLYRIETTES . . . . Kelly Campbell, Lourdes Guzman-Mercado, Mayelyn Perdomo Santos, Natalie Pierre, Idania Quezada, Arianne Recto

DANCERS . . . . .Dezire Duverglas, Tyree Foster, Tenaya Griffin, Jennifer Levine, Anthony Parmer, Genesis Perdomo Santos, Adi Presumé, Ryan Washington

SINGERS . . . . Tamara Pilar Allen, Sarah Bernero, Llewellyn "LC" Connolly, José Dévora, Denton Alexander "Lex" Smith

OLIVIA'S JAZZ FUNERAL PROCESSION . . . . Steve Gluzband, Stafford Hunter, Ben Stapp, Dave Clive,Ronnie Magri, Ric Frank

VIOLA'S INNER MONOLOGUE . . . . .Stefanie Anarumo, Beth Applebaum, Samuel Caraballo, Maleni Chaitoo, Christina Marie Cogswell, Craig Fogel, Reb Grant, Opal Gordon, Shelly Guy, Kimberly Hale, Joyce Hom, Carmen King, Liarra Michelle, Chris Ogren, Christopher Tester, Danica Zielinski

MALVOLIO'S CAN-CAN........Dorian Cervantes, Christina Johnson, Tsubasa Ogawa, Julie Megan Smith, Nobuya Nagahama, Jessica Martineau, Laura Lee Anderson, Rachael Ma, Sarah Conrad, Angela Harriell

SIR TOBY'S DUEL MASTERS.......Ai Ikeda, Irene Liew, Cynthia Eng, Jake Jansen, Brandom Sugiyama, Wendell Millett

SIR TOBY'S DRUM MASTERS.....Yako Miyamoto, Micro Fukuyama, Yuko Ikeshita, Namiko Yamada, Takae Kawabe

ILLYRIANS.....................Melissa Apedo, H. Sebastian Arteta, Noemi Avenancio, Hasaan Bailey, Thomas Barzey, Marc Boone, Adrienne Brammer, Timothy Canady, Carlson Clarke, Micarla Clarke, Michelle Clarke, Brenda Coker, Denisse Cotto, Rosa Downing, Ellie Dunn, Suzie Dunn, Aileen Fraser, Angelica Gaussaint, Osi Gerald, Giovanna Gordon, Bella Gutierrez, Kneeco Hanton, Daejean Heholt, Jaeden Heholt, Josué Hernández, Vivian Kogan, Chan Lai-Tho, Jason Lampert, Aynisa Leonardo, Darr-Lilly, Uwimana Liverpool, Adrian Martinez, Alando McIntyre, Lymarie Monzón, Muriel Moses, Colleen Muhammad, Elsa Newman, Sue Newman, Lizeth Palencia, Louise Parks, Tanais Perdomo Santos, Lucas Phayre-Gonzalez, Ka Keith Puan, Madeline Ramos, Gloria Ranjitsingh, Shannon Rhett, Hector Rivera, Joyce K. Romain, Khalil Romain, David Smith, James P. Stanton, Roslyn Svendsen, Amanda Torres, Melanie Vinson, Catherine Watson, Samantha Williams, Eirene Zanja, Annie Zhao

TWELFTH NIGHT was remounted at the Delacorte Theater, opening on July 17, 2018. The performance was directed by Oskar Eustis and Kwame Kwei-Armah, with music direction by J. Oconer Navarro, sets by Rachel Hauck, costumes by Andrea Hood, lights by John Torres, choreography by Lorin Latarro, and orchestrations by Mike Brun. The Production Stage Manager was Michael Domue. The cast was as follows:

VIOLA	Nikki M. James
COUNTESS OLIVIA	Nanya-Akuki Goodrich
DUKE ORSINO	Ato Blankson-Wood
FESTE	Shaina Taub
MALVOLIO	Andrew Kober
SIR TOBY BELCH	Shuler Hensley
MARIA	Lori Brown-Niang
SIR ANDREW	Daniel Hall
SEBASTIAN	Troy Anthony
ANTONIO	Jonathan Jordan
FABIAN	Patrick J. O'Hare
OFFICIANT (RED ENSEMBLE)	Christine Yvette Lewis
OFFICIANT (BLUE ENSEMBLE)	Aden Munassar
ATTENDANT (RED ENSEMBLE)	Jonpaul Niang
ATTENDANT (BLUE ENSEMBLE)	Benjamin Levine
OFFICERS (RED ENSEMBLE)	Alma L. Hueston, Philip Milio
OFFICERS (BLUE ENSEMBLE)	Eddie Bottoms, Ella Evans
WEDDING SINGER	Vivian Jett
YOUNG CHILD (RED ENSEMBLE)	Zion Finnie-Myers
YOUNG CHILD (BLUE ENSEMBLE)	Fiona Chen

ILLYRIANS Kelly Campbell, JW Guido, Lourdes Guzman-Mercado, Natalie Pierre, Idania Quezada, Siena Rafter, Arianne Recto, Mayelyn Perdomo Santos, Matthew Vazquez

FEMALE UNDERSTUDY	Kim Blanck
MALE UNDERSTUDY	Javier Ignacio

ILLYRIANS (RED ENSEMBLE) . . . . H. Sebastian Arteta, Adrienne Brammer, Brianna Cabrera, Samuel Caraballo, Janet Cardona, Nelson Chimilio, Carlson Clarke, Micarla Clarke, Michelle Clarke, Joseph Crowley, Maggie da Silva, Cora Dennis, Ibrahima Diallo, Laura Dukes, Ellie Dunn, Suzie Dunn, Joel Frost, Pinnacle Garcia, Indigo Gaspard, Julie Geisler, Mersadez George, Barbara Gordon, Giovanna Gordon, Opal Gordon, Aynisa Leonardo, Uwimana Liverpool, Jamie Maleszka, Lucia Mason, Francis Mejia, Karen Murphy, Andrea Olivares, Travis Raeburn, D. Michael Ramos, Genesis Perdomo Santos, Aidan Omar Naranjo Sosa, Sarahi Naranjo Sosa, Ziara Naranjo Sosa, Paul "P-Funk" Stallings, Roslyn Svendsen, Atiya Taylor, Traci, Holly Valentine, Dorothy Vazquez, Nicholas Watson, Tar-Shay Margaret Williams, Tommy Williams, Annie Zhao, Yuan Ming Zhao

ILLYRIANS (BLUE ENSEMBLE) . . . . . Monique Arrucci, Thomas Barzey, Clarimar Capellan, Chloe Chen, Irene Chen, Stephanie Chen, Joycelyn Cunningham, Rosa Downing, Elizabeth Ely, Nanjean Gonzalez, Pierre Graves, Ervin "Easy" Hunt, Antoine Jones, Vivian Kogan, Fatemata Krubally, Jennifer Levine, Shaun Ariel Mapp, Christina Marie, Tionna Martinez, Terri Muuss, Hélène Onserud, Lizeth Palencia, Malik Paris, Louise Parks, Anthony Michael Parmer, Rainer Pasca, Virginia Perry, Eric Pierre, Nancy Pierre, Nancy Hannah Pierre, Naomi Pierre, Adi Présumé, Madeline Ramos, Marcia Rose, Mili Shrestha, David Smith, James P. Stanton, Johan Tejada, Lizbeth Tejada, Regine Tinsley, Losseni Toure, Nisani Walser, Sanira Walser, Catherine Watson, Sally Ann Williams, Magdalen Wilson, Fabian Zarta

CHARACTERS

CAST SIZE

4 principal women, 7 principal men, an ensemble of flexible size. Can work with as a few as 4, as many as hundreds.

PRINCIPAL

VIOLA – a young woman

COUNTESS OLIVIA – a countess in Illyria

DUKE ORSINO – a duke in Illyria

FESTE – a female busking musician, must play piano and, ideally, accordion

MALVOLIO – servant to Olivia

SIR TOBY BELCH – uncle to Olivia

MARIA – lady-in-waiting to Olivia

SIR ANDREW – friend to Toby

SEBASTIAN – male twin to Viola

ANTONIO – a young man, friend to Sebastian

FABIAN – groundskeeper to Olivia

FEATURED ROLES

ILLYRIAN OFFICIANT

ILLYRIAN MAIL-PERSON

ILLYRIAN ATTENDANT – ideally a child

FIRST OFFICER

SECOND OFFICER

TRIO OF HORN PLAYERS

ENSEMBLE

ILLYRIAN TOWNSFOLK – should ideally include people of all ages.

There are many featured lines and solos throughout for ensemble members that may be assigned individually as best suits your production.

SETTING

The action of this play takes place now and always in a mythical city surrounded by water called Illyria. Illyria is here, there, and everywhere. No one is an expert in our Illyria. Our Illyria is not set in any one specific era or locale, rather in an imagined city where all cultures are welcome. Our Illyria is filled with different musical styles – ranging from New Orleans jazz to Motown soul to Broadway showtune to 80s pop – in order to create as inclusive a world as possible. If you wish to perform a version of *Twelfth Night* set in a certain time or place, we suggest you create your own, different adaptation of the Shakespeare play.

Twelfth Night is intended to be performed in one act, without an intermission.

AUTHORS' NOTES

Twelfth Night is a new American musical originally created for Public Works, a radically inclusive program at The Public Theater in New York City that believes "Culture belongs to everyone."

Yes, we originally performed it at the Delacorte Theater in Central Park with a gigantic cast, but we also wanted to make sure we created a vibrant and robust adaptation that could be performed with a cast as small as 15 in a black-box.

We invite you to participate in the Public Works spirit by staging our *Twelfth Night* with your communities, school groups, and institutions across the country and around the globe. This show is flexible and can be produced as a straight-up musical, or you can explode it open by adding large numbers of people to your Illyria. Just as Shakespeare did in his time, our goal is to reflect the world we are living in now and invite all citizens into the creative experience.

MUSICAL NUMBERS

01. Play On . . . . Feste, Viola, Orsino, Illyrians
02. Word on the Street . . . . Illyrians
03. Tell Her . . . . Orsino, Viola
04. If You Were My Beloved . . . . Viola, Olivia, Orsino
05. If You Were My Beloved (Reprise) . . . . Antonio
06. Viola's Soliloquy . . . . Viola
07. You're the Worst . . . . Feste, Andrew, Fabian, Toby,
                                              Maria, Malvolio, Illyrians
08. Is This Not Love? . . . . Feste
09. Count Malvolio (Part I) . . . . Malvolio
09a. Count Malvolio (Part II) . . . . Malvolio, Illyrians
10. I Am She . . . . Olivia, Viola
11. Word on the Street II . . . . Illyrians
12. Count Malvolio (Reprise) . . . . Malvolio
13. What Kind of Man R U Gonna Be? . . . . Viola, Toby,
                                              Andrew, Illyrians
14. Viola's Soliloquy (Reprise) . . . . Viola
15. Greatness . . . . Malvolio
16. Sebastian's Soliloquy . . . . Sebastian, Olivia
17. Word on the Street III . . . . Illyrians
18. Viola's Soliloquy (2nd Reprise) . . . . Viola, Sebastian
19. Tell Her (Reprise) . . . . Orsino, Viola
20. I Am She (Reprise) . . . . Olivia, Viola
21. Malvolio's Exit . . . . Malvolio
22. Is This Not Love? (Reprise) . . . . . . Illyrian Officiant, Company
23. Eyes of Another . . . . Viola, Orsino, Olivia, Sebastian,
                                              Feste, Malvolio, Antonio, Company

Scene One
Opening

[MUSIC 01 – PLAY ON]

(Welcome to the Illyrian town square: A jazz funeral second line parade makes its way onstage.)

*(First, a **TRIO OF HORN PLAYERS** enter, playing a soulful dirge. Next come **ILLYRIAN PALLBEARERS**, carrying a coffin. Next comes **COUNTESS OLIVIA** dressed all in black, in mourning for her deceased brother. She is accompanied by her household chief-of-staff, **MALVOLIO**, and her uncle **SIR TOBY BELCH**, drink in hand. Then comes **DUKE ORSINO**, gazing longingly after **OLIVIA**, his unrequited crush. They are followed by all the **ILLYRIANS**. The funeral dirge comes to a climax.)*

*(**FESTE**, a busking musician, accordion in hand, sits with her band at their regular busking spot in the town square. An **ILLYRIAN**, ideally a child if there is one in the cast, approaches **FESTE** and puts a coin in her tip jar.)*

ILLYRIAN. Feste, if music be the food of love, play on.

FESTE. One, two, one, two, three, four!

*(**FESTE** strikes up the band and leads the **ILLYRIANS** in an upbeat song and dance. Only **OLIVIA** and **ORSINO** are immune to the*

joyful spirit as they each retreat into their own grief.)

FESTE & ILLYRIANS.
IF MUSIC BE THE FOOD OF LOVE, PLAY ON,
PLAY ON!
IF MUSIC BE THE FOOD OF LOVE, PLAY ON!

FESTE.
BLISS AND MISERY,
LET THEM WAIL IN HARMONY,
EVEN WHEN IT SEEMS ALL HOPE IS GONE, PLAY ON!

ILLYRIANS.
PLAY ON!

FESTE & ILLYRIANS.
IF MUSIC BE THE FOOD OF LOVE, PLAY ON,
PLAY ON!
IF MUSIC BE THE FOOD OF LOVE, PLAY ON.

FESTE.
BLOW THAT HORN AND START A RIOT,
TIL MY EARDRUMS NEED A DIET
TIL MY HEARTBEAT STARTS TO HOP.

ORSINO.
I CAN'T TAKE IT NO MORE STOP!

*(**ALL** freeze at the command of the Duke.)*

NO, PLAY ON.

*(**ALL** resume dancing.)*

*(**VIOLA** enters frantically in a crisis, a total wreck – sopping wet, barefoot, covered in seaweed.)*

VIOLA. What country, friend, is this?!

FESTE. This is Illyria, lady!

(**VIOLA** *wanders the streets of Illyria, in shock as everything around her seems to move in slow motion.*)

VIOLA. And what should I do in Illyria?

SEBASTIAN
HAVE YOU SEEN MY BROTHER?
MY TWIN BROTHER, SEBASTIAN
DID HE SWIM TO SHORE TOO?
THE STORM HIT OUR SHIP SO QUICK
NEXT THING I KNEW IT SPLIT IN TWO
DID HE DROWN? OR DID I?
IS THIS WHERE YOU GO WHEN YOU DIE? ILLYRIA?
WHO GOVERNS HERE IN ILLYRIA?

FESTE & ILLYRIANS.
POOR ORSINO! OUR LOVESICK DUKE.
POOR ORSINO!

ILLYRIAN MOM.
WHAT A STUD!

HER LITTLE KID. (*Grossed out by her mom's crush.*)
EW, PUKE!

ORSINO.
THE LADY WON'T LOVE ME BACK.
NO, NO, THE LADY WON'T LOVE ME BACK.
SHE PASSED ME BY SO PROUDLY
IT'S KILLING ME LOUDLY.
THE LADY WON'T LOVE ME BACK.
HOW CAN I GET THE LADY TO LOVE ME BACK?
OH, OH OLIVIA.

VIOLA.
WHO'S OLIVIA?

FESTE & ILLYRIANS.
POOR OLIVIA!
OUR GRIEF-STRICKEN COUNTESS.

VIOLA.

WHO DIED?

FESTE & ILLYRIANS.

HER BROTHER.

VIOLA.

HER BROTHER.

OLIVIA.

EV'RYONE SAYS MOVE ON, OLIVIA.

YOU'VE GOT TO PLAY ON, OLIVIA.

BUT IT FEELS LIKE MY HEART'S WITHDRAWN.

OLIVIA & VIOLA.

HOW WILL I EVER PLAY ON?

VIOLA.   Oh that I served that lady!

ILLYRIAN #1.

YEAH, THE ODDS OF THAT ARE SLIM TO NONE.

ILLYRIAN #2.

OLIVIA WON'T SEE ANYONE.

ILLYRIAN #3.

BUT ORSINO'S HIRING!

VIOLA.

I'LL APPLY!

FESTE.

HE ONLY HIRES MEN.

ILLYRIAN #4.

NEVERMIND THEN.

ILLYRIAN #5.

GOOD LUCK!

FESTE & ILLYRIANS #1-5.

BYE!

VIOLA. *(In soliloquy.)*
MY BROTHER IS THE ONE WHO KNOWS WHAT TO DO.
WHERE WOULD HE GO IN MY SHOELESS SHOES?
WELL, WHAT IF I STEP INTO HIS INSTEAD?
GET THIS JOB, GET FED, A ROOF OVER MY HEAD.

A BASTION OF SECURITY
TIL SEBASTIAN IS RETURNED TO ME
OR THEY FIND HIM UNDER THE SEA.
OH DISGUISE, MAKE THEM SEE
WHAT KIND OF MAN I'VE GOTTA BE!

*(**VIOLA** runs off, with an idea in hand.)*

ALL.
IF MUSIC BE THE FOOD OF LOVE, PLAY ON, PLAY ON.
IF MUSIC BE THE FOOD OF LOVE, PLAY ON.
PLAY MY PAIN, PLAY MY WOE
TIL MY JOY BEGINS TO GROW.
CLAP YOUR HANDS, START TO SWAY
TIL YOUR WORRIES MELT AWAY.

*(**VIOLA** re-enters, now dressed as a man, and joins in the celebration.)*

VIOLA.
BE A MAN AMONG MEN
TIL MY SOUL IS WHOLE AGAIN.

ALL.
TIL OUR AGONY BE GONE

GROUP ONE.
PLAY ON!

GROUP TWO.
PLAY ON!

GROUP ONE.
PLAY ON!

GROUP TWO.
> PLAY ON!

ALL.
> PLAY ON!

VIOLA.
> PLAY ON!

> *(All exit except* **FESTE** *who stays behind with the band, taking her spot at her busking piano. The band plays:)*

[MUSIC 01a – PLAY ON PLAYOFF]

Scene Two
Olivia's Courtyard

*(**TOBY** drunkenly sings an off-key strain of "Play On," banging an empty bottle like a drum. Several **ILLYRIANS** hang out nearby.)*

TOBY. "If music be the fool of love, play on!"

*(**MARIA**, Olivia's housekeeper, enters.)*

Maria! What a plague means my niece, to take the death of her brother thus? I am sure care's an enemy to life.

MARIA. By my troth, Sir Toby, your niece, my lady Olivia, takes great exceptions to your ill hours. You must confine yourself within the modest limits of order.

TOBY. Confine! I'll confine myself no finer than I am. These clothes are good enough to drink in!

MARIA. That drinking will undo you. I heard Olivia talk of it yesterday, and of a foolish knight that you brought in here to be her wooer.

TOBY. Who, Sir Andrew Aguecheek?

MARIA. Ay, he. He's a very fool.

TOBY. Fie, that you'll say so! He hath all the good gifts of nature.

MARIA. He's drunk nightly in your company!

TOBY. With drinking healths to my niece. Here comes Sir Andrew Agueface!

*(**SIR ANDREW** enters.)*

ANDREW. Sir Toby Belch! How now, Sir Toby Belch!

TOBY. Sweet Sir Andrew!

MARIA. Fare you well, gentlemen.

> (**MARIA** *exits.*)

TOBY. O knight thou lackest a cup of canary. When did I see thee so put down?

> (**TOBY** *pours him a drink.*)

ANDREW. Never in your life, I think. I'll ride home tomorrow, Sir Toby.

TOBY. Pourquoi, my dear knight?

ANDREW. Your niece, Olivia, will not be seen; or if she be, It's four to one she'll none of me.
The Duke Orsino himself here hard by woos her.

TOBY. She'll none o' the Duke. I have heard her swear't. Tut, there's life in't, man.

ANDREW. Faith, I'll home tomorrow, Sir Toby.

> (**ANDREW** *turns to leave but* **TOBY** *threatens him with a good time.*)

TOBY. Shall we set about some revels?

ANDREW. I do delight in masques and revels, sometimes altogether.

TOBY. Art thou good at these kickshawses, knight?

ANDREW. Faith, I can cut a caper...

TOBY. Wherefore are these things hid?
Wherefore have these gifts a curtain before them?
Let us see the caper!

> (*The nearby* **ILLYRIANS** *join in the encouragement.*)

ILLYRIAN #5. Let us see it!

ILLYRIANS. Yes, let us see the caper! / Show us the caper! / Yes, Sir Andrew!

(The **ILLYRIANS** *all cheer with support.)*

[MUSIC 01b – LET US SEE THE CAPER]

*(***ANDREW*** *is bashful and resistant at first. But he finally caves in and starts to dance a solo. Everyone responds joyfully to his dancing.)*

ENSEMBLE.
HUH! HUH! HUH!
HUH! HUH! HUH! HUH! HUH! HUH! HUH! HUH!
AHHHH...

TOBY. What is thy excellence in a back-trick, knight? Ay, 'tis strong! 'Tis strong!

ANDREW. I have the back-trick simply as strong as any man in Illyria!

*(***ANDREW*** *does the "back-trick" step and* **TOBY** *and* **ILLYRIANS** *go wild! Now* **ANDREW** *is triumphant.* **TOBY** *and* **ILLYRIANS** *join him in the dance.)*

I'll stay a month longer!

TOBY. Ha, ha – excellent!

*(***ANDREW*** *and* **TOBY** *high-five and exit to continue their revels elsewhere.)*

Scene Three
Town Square

(A group of **ILLYRIANS** *gather to gossip, directly segueing into:)*

[MUSIC 02 – WORD ON THE STREET]

ILLYRIANS.

DID YOU HEAR THE WORD, WORD, WORD
ON THE STREET?
DID YOU HEAR THE WORD, WORD, WORD
ON THE STREET?

ILLYRIAN #6.

ORSINO GOT A BRAND NEW ASSISTANT, DID YA KNOW?

ILLYRIAN #2.

REALLY?

ILLYRIAN #7.

WHO IS HE?

ILLYRIAN #6.

SOME NEW GUY IN TOWN NAMED CESARIO!

ILLYRIANS.

CESARIO??

ILLYRIAN #5.

I HEARD HE'S JUST BEGUN
BUT HE'S ALREADY THE DUKE'S FAVORITE ONE!

ILLYRIAN #4.

I HEARD HE'S GOT A SEXY SMILE.

ILLYRIAN #8.

IF PRETTY BOYS ARE YOUR STYLE.

ILLYRIAN #3.

I LIKE A BIG STRONG HUNK OF A MAN LIKE ORSINO.

ILLYRIAN #1.

NOT MY TYPE.

ILLYRIAN #7.

OR OLIVIA'S TYPE.

ILLYRIANS.

NO ONE'S OLIVIA'S TYPE.

ILLYRIAN #8.

SHE'S STILL IN MOURNING, SHE'S NOT READY TO DATE.

ILLYRIAN #1.

SHE DESERVES A MAN WHO'S WILLING TO WAIT.

ILLYRIAN #2.

BUT THEY'RE MEANT TO BE. IT'S ORSINO AND OLIVIA!

ILLYRIAN #4.

THEY'D MAKE SUCH A POWER COUPLE:

ILLYRIAN #5.

"ORSLIVIA!"

ILLYRIANS.

TELL ME THE WORD, WORD, WORD
ON THE STREET!
DID YOU HEAR THE WORD, WORD, WORD
ON THE STREET?

*(**ORSINO** enters, addressing the **ILLYRIANS**:)*

ORSINO. Who saw Cesario, ho?

*(**VIOLA** enters.)*

VIOLA. On your attendance, my lord, here.

ILLYRIANS. (Gasp!) / Oh my God, it's him! / That's
Cesario!

ORSINO. *(To the **ILLYRIANS**.)* Stand you a while aloof.

*(**ILLYRIANS** exit.)*

ORSINO. Cesario,

[MUSIC 03 – TELL HER]

good youth.

> I'VE ONLY KNOWN YOU FOR THREE DAYS,
> BUT I FEEL LIKE IT'S BEEN YEARS.
> SOMETHIN' ABOUT YOU KID,
> MAKES ME WANNA POUR MY SECRETS IN YOUR EARS.
> YOU'RE THE ONLY ONE WHO KNOWS MY HEART,
> SO YOU'RE PERFECT FOR THIS PART.
>
> I WANT YOU... I NEED YOU...
> TO TELL HER I'M HER MAN.
> I KNOW YOU CAN MAKE HER UNDERSTAND.

VIOLA. I think not so, my lord.

ORSINO. Dear lad, believe it!

> YOU WALK IN THE ROOM
> AND IT'S LIKE SUMMER COMIN' EARLY.
> YOU OPEN YOUR MOUTH
> AND I FEEL TWENTY-TWO AGAIN.
> AND YOUR SMILE...
> HOW COULD SHE SAY NO TO THAT SMILE?
>
> I WANT YOU... I NEED YOU...
> TO TELL HER SHE'S MY GIRL.
> BOY, YOU GOTTA GET HER FOR MY GIRL.
> I WANT YOU...

VIOLA. *(In a high, feminine octave.)*
> SO, SO, YOU WANT ME?

ORSINO.	**VIOLA.** *(Catching herself –*
I NEED YOU...	*in a lower octave.)*
	YOU SURE YOU NEED ME
TO TELL HER SHE'S THE	TO TELL HER?
ONE.	

ORSINO.

> BOY, YOU GOTTA GO AND GET IT DONE,
> 'CAUSE WHEN I TRY TO CHARM HER,
> SHE CAN'T LOOK BEYOND THE ARMOR
> OF A NOBLE DUKE TOO PROUD TO BE BELIEVED.
> BUT SHE'LL LISTEN WHEN YOU ASK,
> 'CAUSE YOU DON'T HAVE THAT MASK.
> YEAH, YOU CAN WEAR YOUR HEART
> RIGHT ON YOUR SLEEVE!

VIOLA. I'll do my best to woo your lady.

ORSINO. Prosper well in this,
And thou shalt live as freely as thy lord,
To call his fortunes thine!

> *(**ORSINO** exits.)*

VIOLA.

> I WANT TO...
> I NEED TO...
> TELL YOU HOW I FEEL.
> I CAN NEVER TELL YOU HOW I FEEL.

Scene Four
Olivia's Courtyard

(**MARIA** *enters and approaches* **FESTE**.)

MARIA. Feste! My lady Olivia will hang thee for thy absence.

FESTE. Let her hang me. Many a good hanging prevents a bad marriage.

MARIA. And that may you be bold to say in your foolery.

FESTE. Well, God give them wisdom that have it. And those that are fools, let them use their talents.

MARIA. Peace, you rogue, no more o' that. Here comes my lady. Make your excuse wisely.

(**MARIA** *exits.*)

(*The* **HORN TRIO** *enters with* **OLIVIA**, *playing the same funeral dirge from before.*)

[MUSIC 03a – OLIVIA'S FANFARE #1]

(*This jazz funeral follows her wherever she goes, signaling her period of grief and heralding her arrivals.*)

(**MALVOLIO** *enters behind them.*)

FESTE. God bless thee, lady!

OLIVIA. (*To the* **HORN TRIO**.) Take the fool away.

FESTE. Do you not hear her, fellows? Take away the lady.

OLIVIA. Fool, I bid them take away you.

FESTE. Good lady, give me leave to prove you a fool.

OLIVIA. Well, for want of other idleness, I'll bide your proof.

FESTE. Good lady, why mournest thou?

OLIVIA. Good fool, for my brother's death.

FESTE. I think his soul is in hell, lady.

OLIVIA. I know his soul is in heaven, fool.

FESTE. The more fool, lady, to mourn for your brother's soul being in heaven.

> (*Even* **OLIVIA** *cracks a smile at Feste's dumb joke.*)

OLIVIA. What think you of this fool, Malvolio? Doth she not mend?

MALVOLIO. Yes, and shall do til the pangs of death shake her.

FESTE. Whoa. Harsh.

MALVOLIO. I marvel your ladyship takes delight in such a barren rascal.

OLIVIA. Oh, you are sick of self-love, Malvolio.

> (**FESTE** *heads back to her busking station as* **MARIA** *enters.*)

MARIA. Madam, there is at the gate a young gentleman much desires to speak with you.

OLIVIA. From the Duke Orsino, is it?

MARIA. I know not, madam: 'tis a fair young man.

OLIVIA. Go you, Malvolio. If it be a suit from the Duke, I am sick, or not at home. What you will, to dismiss it.

> (**MALVOLIO** *and* **MARIA** *exit.*)

> (**TOBY** *enters, singing an off-key strain from "Tell Her," bottle in hand.*)

TOBY. "I want you... I need you...to make me eggs and ham, give me extra jam..."

OLIVIA. Uncle, how have you come so early by this lethargy?

TOBY. Lechery! I defy lechery. There's one at the gate.

*(**TOBY** exits. **MALVOLIO** enters.)*

MALVOLIO. Madam, yond young fellow swears he will speak with you. I told him you were sick. He takes on him to understand so much, and therefore comes to speak with you. I told him you were asleep; he seems to have a foreknowledge of that too, and therefore comes to speak with you. What is to be said to him, lady? He's fortified against any denial.

OLIVIA. What kind o' man is he?

MALVOLIO. Why, of mankind.

OLIVIA. What manner of man?

MALVOLIO. Of very ill manner.
Not yet old enough for a man, nor young enough for a boy.

OLIVIA. Let him approach.

*(**OLIVIA** places a veil over her face. **MALVOLIO** exits.)*

*(**VIOLA** enters.)*

VIOLA. The honorable lady of the house, which is she?

OLIVIA. Speak to me; I shall answer for her. Your will?

VIOLA. Most radiant, exquisite and unmatchable beauty – I pray you, tell me if this be the lady of the house, for I never saw her: I would be loath to cast away my speech, for besides that it is excellently well penned, I have taken great pains to con it.

OLIVIA. Are you a comedian?

VIOLA. Are you the lady of the house?

OLIVIA. I am. What are you? What would you?

VIOLA. Good madam, let me see your face.

OLIVIA. Have you any commission from your lord to negotiate with my face? But we will draw the curtain and show you the picture. Look you, sir, is't not well done?

*(**OLIVIA** removes the veil from her face.)*

VIOLA. Excellently done, if God did all.
I see you what you are, you are too proud;
But, if you were the devil, you are fair.
My lord and master, Orsino loves you.

OLIVIA. How does he love me?

VIOLA. With adorations, fertile tears, and sighs of fire.

OLIVIA. Your lord does know my mind; I cannot love him.

[MUSIC 04 – IF YOU WERE MY BELOVED]

VIOLA. If I did love you in my master's flame,
In your denial I would find no sense;
I would not understand it.

OLIVIA. Why, what would you?

VIOLA.
I WOULD BUILD A CABIN RIGHT AT YOUR GATE
'CAUSE MY HEART WOULD BE CHAINED TO YOUR FLOOR.
I WOULD CALL UP TO YOUR WINDOW
TIL YOU OPENED UP THE DOOR,
IF YOU WERE MY BELOVED.
IF YOU WERE MY BELOVED.

I WOULD WRITE YOU SONGS OF UNANSWERED LOVE
AND SING 'EM LOUD LATE AT NIGHT WITHOUT SHAME.
I WOULD SHOUT IT FROM THE ROOFTOPS,
TIL THE HEAVENS KNEW YOUR NAME,
IF YOU WERE MY BELOVED.

VIOLA.
>IF YOU WERE MY BELOVED.
>IF YOU WERE MY BELOVED.

OLIVIA. What is your parentage?

VIOLA. Above my fortunes, yet my state is well: I am a gentleman.

OLIVIA. Get you to your lord;
>I cannot love him: let him send no more –
>Unless, perchance, you come to me again,
>To tell me how he takes it.

VIOLA. Farewell, fair cruelty.

>(**VIOLA** *exits.*)

OLIVIA.
>OH I FEEL A FEVER RISE IN MY EYES
>FROM THE HEAT OF HIS FACE AS HE PASSED
>OLIVIA, BE CAUTIOUS.
>YOU'RE FALLING FAR TOO FAST!
>COULD HE BE MY BELOVED?
>HE COULD BE MY BELOVED.

What ho, Malvolio!

>(**MALVOLIO** *re-enters.*)

MALVOLIO. Here, madam, at your service.

>(**OLIVIA** *takes a ring off her finger and hands it to* **MALVOLIO.**)

OLIVIA. Run after that same peevish messenger.
>He left this ring behind him; tell him I'll none of it.
>I am not for him.
>If that the youth will come this way tomorrow,
>I'll give him reasons for it: hie thee, Malvolio.

MALVOLIO. Madam, I will.

(**MALVOLIO** *exits.*)

(*A triple soliloquy, sung overlapping:*)

OLIVIA.
I DON'T KNOW
WHAT I'M
DOING,

VIOLA.
I WANT HIS LOVE
BUT I'LL NEVER
WIN IT,
WHILE SHE
COULD HAVE
HIM IN A
MINUTE.

ORSINO.
WHAT WILL SHE
SAY

IS IT JUST LUST...

ISN'T IT IRONIC?

TO THE BOY?
HE'S QUITE
CHARMING,

OR MUST HE BE
MINE?

I HOPE SOME DAY
SHE FALLS
UNREQUITEDLY
HEAD OVER
HEELS
SO SHE CAN SEE

WILL SHE GIVE
ME ANOTHER
COLD
SHOULDER?

C'MON FATE,

HOW IT FEELS!

GIVE ME A SIGN!

OR WILL I FIN'LLY
HOLD HER?

OLIVIA, VIOLA & ORSINO.
I COULD THROW ALL MY SORROW AWAY
AND PLAY JOYFUL TUNES ON REPEAT.

ORSINO.
SO SWEET

OLIVIA, VIOLA & ORSINO.

> ALONE, I'M PUZZLE PIECES,
> BUT I WOULD BE COMPLETE.

OLIVIA.

> IF YOU WERE MY BELOVED.

VIOLA.

> IF YOU WERE MY BELOVED.

ORSINO.

> IF YOU WERE MY BELOVED.

OLIVIA, VIOLA & ORSINO.

> IF YOU WERE MY BELOVED.
> OOH

Scene Five
On the Outskirts of Illyria

(As **VIOLA** *exits,* **SEBASTIAN**, *her twin brother, enters dressed identically to her. He crosses right by her, but they do not see each other.* **ANTONIO** *enters, following* **SEBASTIAN**.*)*

ANTONIO. Roderigo, will you stay no longer? Nor will you not that I go with you?

SEBASTIAN. By your patience, no, Antonio. The malignancy of my fate might perhaps distemper yours. It were a bad recompense for your love to lay any of them on you.

ANTONIO. Let me yet know of you and whither you are bound.

SEBASTIAN. You must know of me then. My name is Sebastian, which I called Roderigo.

ANTONIO. Sebastian.

SEBASTIAN. My father left behind him myself and a sister, both born in an hour.

Before you took me from the breach of the sea was my sister drowned.

ANTONIO. Alas the day!

SEBASTIAN. She bore a mind that envy could not but call fair.

ANTONIO. Pardon me, sir.

SEBASTIAN. O good Antonio, forgive me your trouble.

ANTONIO. Let me be your servant.

SEBASTIAN. If you will not undo what you have done – that is, kill him whom you have recovered – desire it not. I am bound to the Duke Orsino's court in Illyria. Fare you well at once.

(**SEBASTIAN** *exits.*)

ANTONIO. Illyria?

[MUSIC 05 – IF YOU WERE MY BELOVED (REPRISE)]

THERE'S A BOUNTY ON MY HEAD IN THAT TOWN
IT WOULD BE FOOLISH TO FOLLOW YOU THERE
BUT I'LL GLADLY RISK THE DANGER.
I WILL SEEK YOU ANYWHERE
'CAUSE YOU ARE MY BELOVED
YOU ARE MY BELOVED!

(**ANTONIO** *exits, following* **SEBASTIAN.**)

Scene Six
Town Square

(**VIOLA** *enters, followed by* **MALVOLIO**.)

MALVOLIO. Were not you even now with the Countess
Olivia?

VIOLA. Even now, sir.

MALVOLIO. She returns this ring to you, sir. You might
have saved me my pains to have taken it away yourself.
She adds, moreover, that you should put your lord into
a desperate assurance she will none of him. And one
thing more, that you be never so hardy to come again
in your lord's affairs, unless it be to report your lord's
taking of this. Receive it so.

VIOLA. (*Playing along.*) She took the ring of me: I'll none
of it.

MALVOLIO. (*Throwing the ring on the ground.*) Come, sir,
if it be worth stooping for, there it lies in your eye; if
not, be it his that finds it.

(**MALVOLIO** *exits.*)

(**VIOLA** *picks up the ring, bewildered.*)

[MUSIC 06 – VIOLA'S SOLILOQUY]

VIOLA.
WHAT THE...
BUT I NEVER GAVE HER A RING.
SO THEN, WHY'S SHE GIVING ME A RING?

...Oh shit.

WHAT COULD OLIVIA SEE IN ME?
IN CESARIO?
DOES CESARIO HAVE SOMETHING I DIDN'T HAVE BEFORE?
AND WHAT DO I SEE IN ORSINO?

VIOLA.

HE'S SELFISH, DEPRESSED
AND CLEARLY OBSESSED WITH OLIVIA!
BUT HE'S SO DAMN DREAMY,
AND PASSIONATE, TOO.

MY BROTHER IS THE ONE WHO ALWAYS GETS THE GIRL,
AND I'M THE GIRL WHO'S NEVER HAD A CHANCE
TO GET THE GUY.
BUT NOW THAT I'M WEARING THE PANTS,
I'M IN LOVE WITH THE GUY
AND THE GIRL LOVES ME.
WHEN THEY LOOK, WHO DO THEY SEE?

OH DISGUISE, YOU ARE THE DEVIL'S BLESSING,
YOU'VE CAST ME IN THIS STRANGE NEW ROLE.
IS THIS COSTUME GETTING ME WRONG
OR LETTING LOOSE WHAT'S BEEN IN ME ALL ALONG?
DO THESE CLOTHES CONCEAL OR REVEAL MY SOUL?
OH DISGUISE, WHICH OF US IS IN CONTROL?

MY BROTHER IS THE ONE WHO EV'RYBODY EYES.
I NEVER UNDERSTOOD IT, 'CAUSE HE BARELY TRIES.
BUT NOW THAT I'VE WALKED MILES IN HIS SHOES,
I FIN'LLY SEE WHY HE NEVER SEEMS TO LOSE!

I FEEL SO SEEN AS A GUY!
PEOPLE MOVE ASIDE WHEN I WALK BY.
I FELT SO VEILED AS A GIRL,
INVISIBLE TO THE WORLD.
IT WAS ALWAYS "LOOK, DON'T TOUCH,"
NO IT DIDN'T SUIT ME MUCH.
WHY HAS THIS POWER IN ME
NEVER BEEN GIVEN A CHANCE?
IS IT AS SIMPLE AS PUTTING ON A PAIR OF PANTS?

OH DISGUISE, YOU ARE THE DEVIL'S BLESSING,
YOU'VE CAST ME IN THIS WILD, NEW ROLE.

DOES THIS FRESHLY FEARLESS SKIN
FIT ME BETTER THAN THE ONE I'VE BEEN IN?
AM I FINALLY SHEDDING A WELL-WORN SHAWL?
AM I MORE MYSELF NOW THAT I'M NOT MYSELF AT ALL?

(She catches sight of herself in a mirror, and removes her disguise.)

IF I'M A GIRL AGAIN,
WOULD HE CARE WHAT I HAVE TO SAY ANYMORE?
OR WOULD I JUST BE A PRIZE FOR HIM TO WIN?
WOULD I EVEN BE A WOMAN HE'D ADORE?
WOULD I BE ENOUGH IN MY OWN SKIN?

OR WAS THE OLD ME ONLY A COSTUME, TOO?
WHO AM I BESIDES HOW I LOOK TO YOU?
WHO AM I BESIDES HOW I LOOK TO YOU?
WHO AM I?

OH DISGUISE, YOU ARE THE DEVIL'S BLESSING,
YOU'VE LEFT ME UNDRESSED
AND SECOND-GUESSING HOW.
I'VE SEEN MYSELF FROM BOTH SIDES NOW.
IS IT HALF OF EACH BRINGING LOVE MY WAY?
OH DISGUISE,

*(**VIOLA** puts her disguise back on.)*

MAYBE JUST ONE MORE DAY.

Scene Seven
Late Night in Olivia's Courtyard

(**TOBY** *and* **ANDREW** *enter with a group of* **ILLYRIANS**, *including* **FABIAN**. *They're having a messy, unauthorized party late at night at Olivia's house. The band plays:*)

[MUSIC 06a – ON THE STREET (TRANSITION)]

(**TOBY** *approaches* **FESTE** *at her busking station.*)

TOBY. Feste! Feste!

There is sixpence for you.

Let's have a song!

FESTE. Would you have a love song or a song of good life?

ANDREW. I care not for good life.

TOBY. Let our song be "Thou Knave"!

FESTE. I shall be constrained in it to call thee knave, Toby.

TOBY. Begin, Fool!

(**FESTE** *unleashes her accordion.*)

[MUSIC 07 – YOU'RE THE WORST]

FESTE.

MY FRIEND, I KNOW YOU BEST,

BUT I LIKE YOU ANYWAY.

AND A REAL PAL TELLS THE TRUTH,

WARTS AND ALL THE WAY.

INSTEAD OF A PHONY TOAST,

YOU DESERVE AN HONEST ROAST.

SO LET'S ALL RAISE A GLASS,

TO MY FAVORITE PAIN IN THE ASS.

To Sir Toby Belch!

ALL. To Sir Toby Belch!

FESTE.
>YOU'RE THE WORST!
>YOU'RE A SLOUCH.
>A POTATO GONE BAD ON THE COUCH.

ANDREW.
>YOU'RE A LEECH,
>AND A GLUT.

FABIAN.
>AND YOUR EGO'S AS BIG AS YOUR GUT.

FESTE.
>YOUR BURPS ARE SO FAMOUS
>THEY'RE PART OF YOUR NAME.
>YOU SMELL LIKE PERFUME
>MADE OF WHISKEY AND SHAME.
>SO LET ME TELL YOU FIRST,
>THAT YOU ARE THE WORST!

ALL.
>YOU ARE THE WORST!

FESTE.
>WHO IS THE WORST?

ALL.
>TOBY'S THE WORST!

ANDREW. A mellifluous voice, as I am true knight.

TOBY. To Sir Andrew!

ALL. To Sir Andrew!

TOBY.
>YOU'RE THE WORST,

ALL.
>YOU'RE THE WORST!

TOBY.

YOU'RE A DRAG!

CAN'T FLIRT YOUR WAY OUT OF A PAPER BAG.

FESTE.

YOU'RE A WIMP,

AND NAIVE.

IT SAYS GULLIBLE THERE ON YOUR SLEEVE

ANDREW. *(Checking his sleeve.)* Where?!

TOBY.

SO YOU THINK YOU CAN DANCE

BUT TRUST ME, YOU CAN'T.

FABIAN.

YOU'VE THE WIT OF A TOAD AND THE BRAIN OF AN ANT.

FESTE, FABIAN & TOBY.

SO, LET ME TELL YOU FIRST,

THAT YOU ARE THE WORST!

ALL.

YOU ARE THE WORST!

FESTE.

WHO IS THE WORST?

ALL.

ANDREW'S THE WORST!

*(**MARIA** enters.)*

MARIA. What a caterwauling do you keep here! For the love o' God, peace!

TOBY. To Maria!

ALL. To Maria!

TOBY.

YOU'RE THE WORST!

ALL.

YOU'RE THE WORST!

TOBY.

YOU'RE THE...

Actually, Maria's kind of the best, I got nothing. Anyone?

ALL. *(Murmuring in agreement.)* No, yeah, she's pretty great. / Can't think of anything readily. / Hmm, you're right.

TOBY. To Feste!

ALL. To Feste!!

TOBY.

YOU'RE THE WORST!

ALL.

YOU'RE THE WORST!

ANDREW.

YOU'RE A FOOL!!

FESTE. Clever.

FABIAN.

AND YOU THINK YOU'RE JUST TOO COOL FOR SCHOOL

TOBY.

YOU'RE A SMART-ASS!

ANDREW.

A SMART-ASS!

TOBY.

AND A BUM.

ANDREW.

BUM-BUM!

FABIAN.

AND YOUR JOKES ARE ALL PRETTY DUMB.

ANDREW.

NOW WHO'S DUMB?

TOBY.

YOU TRY TOO SINCERELY TO PLEASE EVERY CROWD
AND YOU PLAY THE ACCORDION FOR CRYING OUT LOUD!
SO LET ME TELL YOU FIRST
THAT YOU ARE THE WORST!

ALL.

YOU ARE THE WORST!

TOBY.

WHO IS THE WORST?

ALL.

FESTE'S THE WORST!

TOBY. No, I'm the worst!

ANDREW. No, I'm the worst!!

TOBY. No, I'm the worst!

ANDREW. No, I'm the worst!!

MARIA. Ladies, ladies, you're both pretty much the worst.

ALL.

GOOD FRIENDS HAVE X-RAY VISION
THEY SEE THROUGH THE MASK THAT YOU WEAR.
GOOD FRIENDS LAUGH IN DERISION
TO SHOW YOU THAT THEY CARE!

(**MALVOLIO** *enters, cutting off the music like
a record scratch.*)

MALVOLIO. My masters, are you mad? Do you make an
alehouse of my lady's house? Is there no respect of
place, persons, nor time in you?

TOBY. To Malvolio!

ALL. To Malvolio!

MALVOLIO. *(Flattered.)* To me?

TOBY.

YOU'RE THE WORST!

ALL.

YOU'RE THE WORST!

MALVOLIO. The worst?!

TOBY.

YOU'RE A FROWN.

MALVOLIO. Have you no manners?

TOBY.

AND YOU POOP EVERY PARTY IN TOWN.

MALVOLIO. This is much credit to you!

TOBY.

YOU'RE A SNOB.

MALVOLIO. Sir Toby, I must be –

TOBY.

AND A SNITCH.

MALVOLIO. I must be round with you –

TOBY.

A HIGH-HORSE RIDIN' SON OF A /

MARIA. *(Trying to muffle **TOBY**'s profanity in front of **MALVOLIO.**)*

/ GUN!

TOBY.

YOU THINK JUST 'CAUSE YOU NEVER HAVE ANY FUN

ANDREW.

THAT EVERYONE ELSE SHALL ALSO HAVE NONE!

TOBY.

I'M SURE I'M NOT THE FIRST TO SAY
YOU'RE THE WORST!

ALL.

YOU ARE THE WORST!

MALVOLIO. I'm *not* the worst!

ALL.

MALVOLIO'S THE WORST!

FESTE. He's actually the worst though.

ALL.

YOU ARE THE WORST!
LET'S HEAR IT FOR YOUR TRUE FRIENDS,
WHO TELL YA STRAIGHT TO YOUR FACE.
THAT YOU'RE A DISGRACE!

HEAR HEAR!

> *(Just before the final button of the song,* **MALVOLIO** *pulls the plug on the stereo or turns off the lights, abruptly cutting off the number. He shoos them away, ending the party, and storms off, muttering things like "Out, out all of you!" All groan and start to leave.)*

MARIA. *(Calling after* **MALVOLIO**.*)* Go shake your ears!

ANDREW. Oh how I would love to challenge Malvolio to the field and then break promise with him and make a fool of him!

TOBY. Do it, knight. I'll write thee a challenge: or I'll deliver thy indignation to him by word of mouth.

MARIA. Sweet Sir Toby, be patient for tonight. For Monsieur Malvolio, let me alone with him.

TOBY. What wilt thou do?

MARIA. I will drop in his way some obscure epistles of love. I can write very like my lady Olivia.

TOBY. Excellent! I smell a device.

ANDREW. I have't in my nose too.

TOBY. He shall think, by the letters that thou wilt drop, that they come from my niece, and that she's in love with him.

MARIA. My purpose is indeed a horse of that color.

TOBY. And your horse now would make him an ass!

MARIA. Ass, I doubt not. For this night, to bed, and dream on the event.

(**MARIA** *exits as the band plays.*)

[MUSIC 07a – YOU'RE THE WORST (TAG)]

TOBY. She's a beagle, true-bred, and one that adores me. What of that?

ANDREW. I was adored once too.

TOBY. Come, come, I'll go burn some sack. 'Tis too late to go to bed now. Come, knight. Come, knight.

(*They exit.*)

Scene Eight
Late Night in Town Square

(ORSINO and VIOLA enter.)

ORSINO. Feste, give me some music.

(The band begins to play:)

[MUSIC 07b – BELOVED (UNDERSCORE)]

Come hither, boy, good Cesario: if ever thou shalt love,
In the sweet pangs of it remember me;
How dost thou like this tune?

VIOLA. It gives a very echo to the seat
Where Love is throned.

ORSINO. Thou dost speak masterly:
My life upon't, young though thou art, thine eye
Hath stayed upon some favor that it loves:
Hath it not, boy?

VIOLA. A little, by your favor.

ORSINO. What kind of woman is't?

VIOLA. Of your complexion.

ORSINO. She is not worth thee, then. What years, i' faith?

VIOLA. About your years, my lord.

ORSINO. Too old by heaven.
O Feste, play that old song we heard last night.
Methought it did relieve my passion much.
I prithee, sing.

(FESTE sings from the piano:)

[MUSIC 08 – IS THIS NOT LOVE?]

FESTE.

> I CAN TELL YOU ANYTHING, MY FRIEND
> EXCEPT HOW I FEEL ABOUT YOU,
> 'CAUSE I KNOW YOU DON'T RETURN IT.
> THOUGH AIN'T IT OBVIOUS, MY FRIEND,
> I'M NOT MYSELF AROUND YOU.
> BUT I LIKE WHO I AM TURNING INTO.
> 'CAUSE I BEEN MISSING PARTS OF ME.
> BUT WHEN I'M WITH YOU, I FEEL PUT BACK TOGETHER
>
> AND I KNOW I SHOULDN'T SAY IT.
> BUT BABY, WHY DON'T YOU SEE IT?
>
> IS THIS NOT LOVE?
> IS THIS NOT LOVE THAT I FEEL FOR YOU?
> DO YOU FEEL IT TOO?
> IS THIS NOT LOVE?
> IS THIS NOT LOVE THAT WE'RE FEELING?
> IS THIS NOT LOVE?

ORSINO. Once more, Cesario,

> Get thee to yond same sovereign cruelty. Tell her my love.

VIOLA. But if she cannot love you, sir?

ORSINO. I cannot be so answered.

FESTE.

> I'M DESPONDENCE DRESSED LIKE CONFIDENCE,
> A LAMB IN LION'S CLOTHES.
> I WANNA HOLD YOU SO BAD
> AND I'M NOT THE ONE YOU CHOSE.
> BUT SOMETIMES YOUR EYES CATCH MINE,
> AND I DARE THINK IT.
> OH I THINK YOU KNOW IT.
>
> IS THIS NOT LOVE?
> IS THIS NOT LOVE THAT I FEEL FOR YOU?
> DO YOU FEEL IT TOO?

FESTE.

> IS THIS NOT LOVE?
> IS THIS NOT LOVE THAT WE'RE FEELING?
> IS THIS NOT LOVE?

VIOLA. Say that some lady, as perhaps there is,
Hath for your love as great a pang of heart
As you have for Olivia: you cannot love her;
You tell her so; must she not then be answered?

ORSINO. Make no compare
Between that love a woman can bear me
And that I owe Olivia.

VIOLA. Ay, but I know –

ORSINO. What dost thou know?

VIOLA. Too well what love women to men may owe:
In faith, they are as true of heart as we.
My father had a daughter loved a man
As it might be, perhaps, were I woman,
I should your lordship.

ORSINO. And what's her history?

VIOLA. She never told her love. She pined in thought,
And with a green and yellow melancholy
She sat like patience on a monument,
Smiling at grief. Was not this love indeed?

ORSINO. But died thy sister of her love, my boy?

VIOLA. ...I know not.

FESTE.

> WILL I DIE WITHOUT SAYING A THING?
> WILL I WAIT HERE FOR YEARS SILENTLY?
> OR WILL I RISK IT ALL,
> LAY BARE MY HEART,

AND SAY IT BABY,
OH I GOTTA SAY IT BABY.

IS THIS NOT LOVE?
IS THIS NOT LOVE THAT I FEEL FOR YOU?
OH, I KNOW YOU FEEL IT, TOO.

IS THIS NOT LOVE?
IS THIS NOT LOVE THAT WE'RE FEELING?
WE'RE FEELIN',
I KNOW WE'RE FEELIN' IT, YEAH,

IS THIS NOT LOVE?
IS THIS NOT LOVE?
IS THIS NOT LOVE?
IS THIS NOT...

VIOLA. Sir, shall I to this lady?

ORSINO. To her in haste. Give her this jewel.

>   (**VIOLA** *exits.*)

>   *(Offering a coin to* **FESTE**.*)* There's for thy pains.

FESTE. *(For once, refusing the coin.)* No pains, sir. I take
pleasure in it.

Scene Nine
Malvolio's Fantasy

(**TOBY** and **ANDREW** enter with **FABIAN**, who they have enlisted in their scheme. As always, **TOBY** is singing an off-key strain of the previous song.)

TOBY. "Is this not Dove? Is this not Dove that I smell on you? Do you smell it too?"

Come thy ways, Signior Fabian!

FABIAN. Nay, I'll come! If I lose a scruple of this sport, let me be boiled to death with melancholy.

TOBY. Wouldst thou not be glad to have the rascally sheep-biter come by some notable shame?

FABIAN. I would exult, man!

TOBY. Here comes the little villain!

(**MARIA** enters.)

MARIA. Get you all three into the boxtree: Malvolio's coming down this walk. Observe him, for the love of mockery, for I know this letter will make a contemplative idiot of him. Here comes the trout that must be caught with tickling.

(They all hide and watch the following. **MALVOLIO** enters.)

[MUSIC 09 – COUNT MALVOLIO (PART I)]

MALVOLIO.
IT ALL COMES DOWN TO LUCK
IN THIS WILD, WICKED WORLD.
BUT LUCK DOESN'T HAVE INFALLIBILITY.

FOR LUCK HAD THE NERVE
TO MAKE ME ONE WHO SERVES
WHEN IT'S PLAIN TO SEE I OUGHT TO BE NOBILITY.

EVEN THE COUNTESS TREATS ME
WITH SUPERIOR RESPECT.
I'M CLEARLY HER FAVORITE IN THE HOUSE.
SHE HINTED ONCE THAT SHOULD SHE EVER MARRY,
SHE HOPES SOMEONE LIKE ME WOULD BE HER SPOUSE.
SO, WHAT'S THE LIKELY THEORY TO ESPOUSE?

I COULD BE COUNT MALVOLIO!
LORD OF THE ESTATE.
DRESSED IN ALL THE FINEST SILK
AND MASTER OF MY FATE.
I'D SUMMON ALL MY MINIONS
IN A MOST MAJESTIC TONE,
THEN ONCE THEY ALL ARRIVED
I'D TELL THEM, "LEAVE ME ALONE!"

IMAGINE COUNT MALVOLIO,
MARRIED UP AND UP.
WATCHING ALL MY FORTUNES AS THEY GREW.
THEY'LL ALL WISH THEY'D BEEN NICE
ONCE I RE-LOAD THE DICE,
WHEN I FINALLY GET MY DUE.

> (*A group of* **ILLYRIANS** *enter as* **MALVOLIO**'s *imaginary "staff" in his dream world dancing with him, enacting his fantasy along with him for the rest of the number.*)

I'D SEND SEVEN SERVANTS OFF TO FETCH MY UNCLE TOBY.
THEN I'D WAIT THERE WITH A MOST IMPATIENT FROWN.
I'D FIDDLE WITH MY DIAMOND-STUDDED WRISTWATCH,
AS I LOUNGE UPON A BED OF FLUFFY DOWN.
THEN TOBY WOULD APPROACH ME WITH A CURTSY,
I'D EXTEND MY REGAL HAND FOR HIM TO KISS.

MALVOLIO.
> BUT INSTEAD OF MY CUSTOMARY COURTESY,
> I'D INDUBITABLY LECTURE HIM LIKE THIS:
> "NOW THAT I'M MARRIED TO THE COUNTESS,
> AT LAST IT IS MY RIGHT TO SPEAK THE TRUTH.
> YOU MUST AMEND YOUR DRINKING AND CAROUSING,
> AND THAT ANDREW FRIEND OF YOURS MUST GO!
> HE'S SIMPLY UNCOUTH!"
>
> AND HE'LL SAY: "COUNT MALVOLIO,
> PLEASE FORGIVE MY FLAWS.
> I'M JUST A LOUSY LIAR
> WHO THINKS HE'S ABOVE THE LAWS.
> IF ONLY YOU COULD TEACH ME HOW TO BE SO REFINED!"
> BUT I'D SAY:
> "SORRY TOBY,
> THERE'S NO HOPE FOR YOUR VULGAR MIND!"
>
> JUST PICTURE COUNT MALVOLIO,
> HONORED AND ADORED.
> MY DESTINY WOULD ALL BE COMING TRUE
> THEY'LL ALL WISH THEY'D BEEN SWEET,
> WELL THEY CAN KISS MY FEET
> WHEN I FINALLY GET MY DUE!

> *(An* **ILLYRIAN MAIL-PERSON** *enters and hands* **MALVOLIO** *a letter, then exits.)*

What have we here?

MARIA. Now is the woodcock near the gin.

MALVOLIO. By my life, this is my lady's hand.

(Reads.) "To the unknown beloved, this, and my good wishes:"

> *(***MALVOLIO** *opens the letter.)*

– her very phrases! To whom should this be?

(Reads.) "Jove knows I love:
But who? Lips, do not move;
No man must know."

No man must know. What follows? *No man must know*: if this should be thee, Malvolio?

(Reads.) "I may command where I adore;
But silence with bloodless stroke my heart doth gore:
'M, O, A, I,' doth sway my life."

TOBY. Excellent wench, say I!

MALVOLIO. *"M, O, A, I," doth sway my life.* Let me see, let me see. *I may command where I adore.* Why, she may command me: I serve her; she is my lady. What should that alphabetical position portend? If I could make that resemble something in me, – Softly! "M, O, A, I," –

TOBY. O, ay, make up that:

MALVOLIO. "M," – Malvolio; "M," – why, that begins my name.

MARIA. Did not I say he would work it out?

MALVOLIO. "M," – but then there is no consonancy in the sequel; "A" should follow but "O" does.

FABIAN. And "O" shall end, I hope.

MALVOLIO. And then "I" comes behind. "M, O, A, I;" every one of these letters are in my name.

Soft! here follows prose.

TOBY. I could marry this wench for this device.

MALVOLIO. *(Reads.)* "If this fall into thy hand, revolve. In my stars I am above thee; but be not afraid of greatness: some are born great, some achieve greatness, and some have greatness thrust upon 'em. Be opposite with a kinsman, surly with servants. Remember who commended thy yellow stockings, and wished to see thee ever cross-gartered: I say, remember. If thou entertainest my love, let it appear in thy smiling; dear my sweet, I prithee. Farewell.

Signed:

The Fortunate-Unhappy!"

(Music resumes for:)

[MUSIC 09a – COUNT MALVOLIO (PART II)]

I KNOW I WASN'T DREAMING
OR GETTING CARRIED AWAY,
MY LADY TRULY LOVES ME,
HER MISSIVE'S PLAIN AS DAY!
THE CLUES ARE ADDING UP,
THE LETTERS IN MY NAME.
NOW ALL I HAVE TO DO IS PLAY HER GAME!

THEN I'LL BE COUNT MALVOLIO,
IF I PLAY ALONG.
ACT SURLY TO THE SERVANTS
AND TELL TOBY THAT HE'S WRONG.
I'LL SPORT MY YELLOW STOCKINGS
AND CROSS-GARTER EVERY LACE
AND ALWAYS WEAR A MONUMENTAL SMILE ON MY FACE!

TIL I AM COUNT MALVOLIO,
I WILL ACE EACH TEST
MY FORTUNATE UNHAPPY PUTS ME TO.
MY INSTRUCTIONS ARE CLEAR,
SO THE DAY'S DRAWING NEAR,
WHEN I'LL FINALLY GET MY DUE!

*(Dance break with the **ILLYRIANS** as **MALVOLIO**'s imaginary staff!)*

I SHALL BE

MALVOLIO & ILLYRIANS.
> COUNT MALVOLIO,

MALVOLIO.
> BY THE GRACE OF JOVE!
> I THANK MY LUCKY STARS FOR COMING THROUGH.
> I'LL DO ALL THAT SHE SAID
> AND THEN WHEN WE ARE WED,
> I WILL FINALLY GET,
> YES I'LL FINALLY GET MY DUE!

ILLYRIANS.
> YOU'LL GET YOUR DUE!

MALVOLIO.
> MY DUE!

ILLYRIANS.
> YOU'LL GET YOUR DUE!

MALVOLIO.	**ILLYRIANS.**
MY DUE!	YOUR DUE!

(All exit as the band plays:)

[MUSIC 09b – COUNT MALVOLIO PLAYOFF]

*(**MALVOLIO**'s fantasy world dissipates and he is alone again. He exits.)*

Scene Ten
Olivia's Courtyard

*(**VIOLA** enters and approaches **FESTE** and the band.)*

VIOLA. Save thee, friend and thy music. I warrant thou art a merry person and carest for nothing.

FESTE. Not so, sir. I do care for something. But in my conscience, I do not care for you.

VIOLA. Art not thou the Lady Olivia's fool? I saw thee late at the Duke Orsino's.

FESTE. Foolery, sir, does walk about the orb like the sun. It shines everywhere.

> *(**FESTE** holds out her tip jar. **VIOLA** drops a coin in.)*

VIOLA. There's expenses for thee.

FESTE. Now Jove, in his next commodity of hair, send thee a beard!

VIOLA. By my troth, I'll tell thee, I am almost sick for one, though I would not have it grow on my chin.

> *(**OLIVIA** enters, accompanied by the **HORN TRIO**, playing:)*

[MUSIC 09c – OLIVIA'S FANFARE #2]

OLIVIA. What is your name?

VIOLA. Cesario is your servant's name, fair princess.

OLIVIA. You're servant to the Duke Orsino, youth.

VIOLA. And he is yours, and his must needs be yours.

OLIVIA. For him, I think not on him.

VIOLA. Dear lady, I come to whet your gentle thoughts on his behalf.

OLIVIA. Give me leave, beseech you.

[MUSIC 10 – I AM SHE]

I HAVE A CONFESSION TO MAKE.
I SENT YOU A RING,
IT WAS A STUPID MISTAKE.
I WAS DESPERATE FOR ANY EXCUSE
TO GET TO SEE YOU AGAIN
OH GOD I'M EMBARRASSED
YOU PROBABLY THINK I'M INSANE
DO YOU THINK I'M INSANE?

VIOLA.

I...

OLIVIA.

IT MUST BE SO OBVIOUS,
ISN'T IT OBVIOUS?
I CAN NO LONGER CONTAIN IT.

I'VE BEEN SHIELDING MY FEELINGS AS I GRIEVE,
BUT NOW I'M WEARING MY HEART ON MY SLEEVE.
AND SAYING YOU SEE ME FOR WHO I REALLY AM,
MY SHAME AND MY PRIDE.
I JUST CAN'T HIDE FROM YOU.
SO PUT ME OUT OF MY MISERY

'CAUSE I AM YOUR WOMAN
I AM SHE.
I AM YOUR WOMAN.
I AM SHE.

VIOLA.

I PITY YOU.

OLIVIA.

BUT PITY IS COMPASSION

OLIVIA.

SO THAT MEANS YOU MUST FEEL PASSION FOR ME.

VIOLA.

NOT EXACTLY.

OLIVIA.

THEN TELL ME PLEASE,

WHAT YOU HONESTLY THINK OF ME NOW?

VIOLA.

I THINK YOU'RE FOOLING YOURSELF.

OLIVIA.

THEN SO ARE YOU.

VIOLA.

OH HONEY, IF ONLY YOU KNEW.

VIOLA & OLIVIA.

I WISH THAT YOU'D SEE ME THE WAY I WANT YOU TO.

OLIVIA.

YOUR LOVER.

VIOLA.

YOUR FRIEND!

OLIVIA.

YOU'RE SEXY WHEN YOU YELL.

OLIVIA & VIOLA.

SO PUT ME OUT OF MY MISERY

OLIVIA.

'CAUSE I AM YOUR WOMAN.

VIOLA.

NOT FOR ME.

OLIVIA.

I AM YOUR WOMAN.

VIOLA.
> YOU'LL NEVER BE.

OLIVIA & VIOLA.
> YOU DON'T UNDERSTAND.
> I AM NOT THE PERSON THAT I USED TO BE LATELY.
> TRY AND SEE IT THROUGH MY EYES.

OLIVIA.
> YOU'VE MADE ME FEEL LIKE I CAN START OVER NEW.

VIOLA.
> I WOULDN'T LOVE ME IF I WERE YOU,

OLIVIA.
> BUT I DO

OLIVIA & VIOLA.
> SO PLEASE,

OLIVIA.   **VIOLA.**
> PUT ME OUT OF MY   PUT ME OUT OF MY
>   MISERY   MISERY

VIOLA.
> 'CAUSE YOU'RE NOT MY WOMAN.

OLIVIA.
> I WILL BE.

VIOLA.
> I GOT NO WOMAN.

OLIVIA.
> I AM SHE.

VIOLA.
> NOT FOR ME.

OLIVIA.
> I AM SHE.

VIOLA.
> NOT FOR ME.

OLIVIA.
> I AM SHE!

VIOLA.
> NOT FOR ME.

OLIVIA.
> I AM SHE.

VIOLA.
> NOT FOR ME.

OLIVIA.
> I AM SHE.

> *(***OLIVIA*** chases ***VIOLA*** offstage as the ***HORN**
> **TRIO*** rushes to keep up.)*

Scene Eleven
Town Square

*(***TOBY, ANDREW,*** and* **FABIAN** *enter.)*

ANDREW. No, faith, I'll not stay a jot longer.

TOBY. Thy reason, dear venom, give thy reason.

ANDREW. Marry, I saw Olivia do more favors to Orsino's servingman Cesario than ever she bestowed upon me. I saw it even now in the orchard!

FABIAN. She did show favor to Cesario in your sight only to exasperate you, to awake your dormouse valor, to put fire in your heart!

TOBY. Why, then, build me thy fortunes upon the basis of valor. Challenge Cesario to fight! Hurt him in eleven places: Olivia shall take note of it; and assure thyself, there is no love-broker in the world can more prevail in man's commendation with woman than report of valor.

FABIAN. There is no way but this, Sir Andrew.

ANDREW. Will either of you bear me a challenge to him?

TOBY. Go, write it in a martial hand; be curst and brief. Go!

*(***ANDREW** *runs off as* **MARIA** *enters.)*

Look where the youngest wren of nine comes!

MARIA. If you will laugh yourself into stitches, follow me. Yond gull Malvolio is in yellow stockings!

TOBY. And cross-gartered?

MARIA. Most villainously!

TOBY. Come, bring us, bring us where he is!

(They exit as the **ILLYRIANS** *enter.)*

[MUSIC 11 – WORD ON THE STREET II]

ILLYRIANS.
> DID YOU HEAR THE WORD, WORD, WORD
> ON THE STREET?
> DID YOU HEAR THE WORD, WORD, WORD
> ON THE STREET?

ILLYRIAN #8.
> THE COUNTESS HAS IT BAD FOR SOMEBODY,
> DID YOU KNOW?

SOME ILLYRIANS.
> OOH!

OTHER ILLYRIANS.
> WHO??

ILLYRIAN #6.
> SHE LIKES THAT NEW KID IN TOWN CALLED CESARIO!

ILLYRIANS.
> WHAT? SCANDAL!

ILLYRIAN #8.
> I DON'T BLAME HER,
> HE MAKES ME WEAK IN THE KNEES.

ILLYRIAN #4.
> ORSINO MUST NOT BE TOO PLEASED.

ILLYRIAN #2.
> ORSINO ONLY WANTS WHAT HE CAN'T HAVE!

ILLYRIAN #3.
> AIN'T THAT THE TRUTH!

ILLYRIAN #8.
> SO DOES OLIVIA.

ILLYRIANS.
> SO DOES OLIVIA.

ILLYRIAN #5.

AND DID YOU HEAR MALVOLIO'S DRESSING UP
AND ACTING CRAZY?

ILLYRIAN #7.

HAS HE GONE CRAZY?

ILLYRIAN #2.

CRAZY FOR OLIVIA!

ILLYRIANS.

EV'RYONE'S CRAZY FOR HER.
SO CRAZY IN LOVE.

ILLYRIAN #4.

UGH, MALVOLIO'S THE WORST!

ILLYRIAN #8.

BUT THEY TEASE HIM SO!

ILLYRIAN #1.

OH, COME ON NOW! HE DESERVES IT, THOUGH!

ILLYRIAN #3.

AND SPEAKING OF CRAZY, THERE'S GONNA BE A FIGHT.
CESARIO VERSUS SIR ANDREW TONIGHT!

SOME ILLYRIANS.

A DUEL?

OTHER ILLYRIANS.

COOL!

ILLYRIANS.

EV'RYONE WANTS WHO THEY DON'T GOT.
AND EV'RYONE'S BEIN' SOMEBODY THEY'RE NOT.
IS IT TRUE?
IS IT TRUE?
WHO'S GONNA END UP WITH WHO?
GIVE ME THE WORD, WORD, WORD
ON THE STREET

ILLYRIANS.
DID YOU HEAR THE WORD, WORD, WORD
ON THE STREET?

(The **ILLYRIANS** *exit.)*

*(***SEBASTIAN** *enters,* **ANTONIO** *follows him on.)*

SEBASTIAN. I would not by my will have troubled you.

ANTONIO. I could not stay behind you, Sebastian. My willing love did spur me forth.

SEBASTIAN. My dear Antonio, I can no other answer make but thanks. What's to do? Shall we go see the relics of this town, Illyria?

ANTONIO. Best first go see your lodging.

SEBASTIAN. I am not weary, and 'tis long to night!

ANTONIO. Would you'd pardon me;
I do not without danger walk these streets;
I was once in a sea-fight against the Duke Orsino. If I be taken in this place, I shall pay dear.

SEBASTIAN. Do not then walk too open.

*(***ANTONIO** *hands* **SEBASTIAN** *his wallet.)*

ANTONIO. Hold, sir, here's my purse.
In the south suburbs, at the Elephant, is best to lodge. There you shall find me.

SEBASTIAN. Why I your purse?

ANTONIO. Haply your eye shall light upon some toy you have desire to purchase.

SEBASTIAN. I'll be your purse-bearer and leave you for an hour.

*(***SEBASTIAN** *and* **ANTONIO** *exit.)*

Scene Twelve
Olivia's Courtyard

*(**OLIVIA** and **MARIA** enter, accompanied by the **HORN TRIO**. Now that **OLIVIA** is in love, she is growing increasingly exasperated by the horns, as they signify her grief. She dismisses them hastily.)*

[MUSIC 11a – OLIVIA'S FANFARE #3]

OLIVIA. I have sent after Cesario: he says he'll come; Where is Malvolio?

MARIA. He's coming, madam; but in very strange manner. He is, sure, possessed.

OLIVIA. Why, what's the matter?

> *(**MALVOLIO** enters, wearing ridiculous yellow stockings.)*

MALVOLIO. Ho, Ho.

OLIVIA. How now, Malvolio!

MALVOLIO. Sweet lady, ho, ho.

OLIVIA. Smilest thou? I sent for thee upon a sad occasion.

MALVOLIO. Sad, lady! I could be sad: this does make some obstruction in the blood, this cross-gartering; but what of that?

OLIVIA. Wilt thou go to bed, Malvolio?

MALVOLIO. To bed? Ay, sweetheart, and I'll come to thee.

MARIA. Why appear you with this ridiculous boldness before my lady?

MALVOLIO. "Be not afraid of greatness:" 'twas well writ.

OLIVIA. What meanest thou by that, Malvolio?

MALVOLIO. "Some are born great," –

OLIVIA. Ha!

MALVOLIO. "Some achieve greatness," –

OLIVIA. What sayest thou?

MALVOLIO. "And some have greatness thrust upon them."

OLIVIA. Heaven restore thee!

MALVOLIO. "Remember who commended thy yellow stockings"

OLIVIA. Thy yellow stockings?

(*Enter* **ILLYRIAN ATTENDANT**, *ideally a kid.*)

ATTENDANT. Madam, Cesario, the young gentleman of the Duke Orsino's is returned: he attends your ladyship's pleasure.

OLIVIA. I'll come to him.

Good Maria, let this fellow be looked to.

(**OLIVIA, MARIA,** *and* **ATTENDANT** *exit.*)

[MUSIC 12 – COUNT MALVOLIO (REPRISE)]

MALVOLIO.
I SHALL BE COUNT MALVOLIO,
SOONER THAN I THOUGHT
THERE'S NOTHING LEFT THAT'S STANDING IN MY WAY
SEE, THE LADY AGREES,
I SHALL BE AS I PLEASE,
AND I'LL FINALLY GET MY DUE!

(**TOBY, FABIAN,** *and* **MARIA** *enter.*)

FABIAN. Here he is, here he is. How is't with you, sir? How is't with you?

MALVOLIO. Go off; I discard you.

MARIA. Lo, how hollow the fiend speaks within him.

TOBY. *(To MARIA.)* Go to, go to; peace, peace; we must deal gently with him: let me alone.

(To MALVOLIO.) How do you, Malvolio? How is't with you? What, man, defy the devil. Consider he's an enemy to mankind.

MALVOLIO. Do you know what you say? Go, hang yourselves all!

(Exit MALVOLIO.)

TOBY. Is't possible?

FABIAN. If this were played upon a stage now, I could condemn it as an improbable fiction.

TOBY. His very genius hath taken the infection of the device, man!

MARIA. Nay, pursue him now, lest the device take air and taint.

TOBY. Come, we'll have him in a dark room and bound. My niece is already in the belief that he's mad. We may carry it thus, for our pleasure and his penance, til our very pastime, tired out of breath, prompt us to have mercy on him.

*(**ANDREW** enters triumphantly, letter in hand.)*

ANDREW. Ah Ha!

MARIA. More matter for a May morning.

*(**MARIA** exits.)*

*(**ANDREW** presents **TOBY** with the letter.)*

ANDREW. Here's the challenge for that brute Cesario, read it.

TOBY. Give me.

(Reads.) "Cesario, whatsoever thou art, thou art but a scurvy fellow."

FABIAN. Good, and valiant.

TOBY. *(To* **ANDREW.***)* If this letter move him not, his legs cannot: I'll give it to him! Go, Sir Andrew. Away!

> *(***ANDREW*** runs off.)*

Now will not I deliver his letter. This letter, being so excellently ignorant, will breed no terror in Cesario. He will find it comes from a clodpole. But, I will deliver his challenge by word of mouth; set upon Sir Andrew a notable report of valor; and drive Cesario into a most hideous opinion of his rage, skill, fury and impetuosity. This will so fright them both that they will kill one another by the look.

> *(***VIOLA*** enters, chased by ***OLIVIA*** and the ***HORN TRIO***, out of breath from trying to keep up with her.)*

[MUSIC 12a – OLIVIA'S FANFARE #4]

FABIAN. Here he comes, with your niece!

OLIVIA. I have said too much unto a heart of stone!

VIOLA. With the same 'havior that your passion bears
Goes on my master's grief.

OLIVIA. I beseech you come again tomorrow. What shall you ask of me that I'll deny?

VIOLA. Nothing but this: your true love for my master.

OLIVIA. How may I give him that which I have given to you?

VIOLA. I will acquit you!

OLIVIA. Well, come again tomorrow!

(**OLIVIA** *exits and* **TOBY** *ambushes* **VIOLA**.)

[MUSIC 13 – WHAT KIND OF MAN R U GONNA BE?]

TOBY.

BOY, THE GAUNTLET HAS BEEN THROWN,
YOU'VE BEEN CHALLENGED TO A FIGHT.
THIS BROTHER'S OUT FOR BLOOD

VIOLA.

WHO WANTS TO FIGHT ME?
WHY?
YOU GOT THE WRONG GUY!

TOBY.

HE THINKS THAT YOU'VE BEEN TALKING SMACK
BEHIND HIS TATTOOED, MUSCLED BACK,
SO NOW HE'S GONNA MAKE YOU PAY

VIOLA.

WHAT KINDA MAN IS HE ANYWAY?

TOBY.

HE'S THE MOST WANTED KILLER IN ILLYRIA
AND HE IS HERE TO BREAK YOUR NECK!

VIOLA.

I FORGOT, I HAVE A THING.
GOTTA GO.
RAIN CHECK?!

TOBY.

STOP BEING SUCH A GIRL
AND ASK YOURSELF

(**TOBY** *recruits all the* **ILLYRIANS** *to help him with the challenge. They train* **VIOLA** *and* **ANDREW** *to get them ready for the epic duel.*)

TOBY & ILLYRIANS.
>WHAT KIND OF MAN ARE YOU GONNA BE?
>WHAT KIND OF MAN ARE YOU GONNA BE?
>ARE YOU GONNA RUN, RUN AWAY?
>OR ARE YOU GONNA SAVE THE DAY?
>WHAT KIND OF MAN ARE YOU GONNA BE?
>WHAT KIND OF MAN ARE YOU GONNA BE?
>ARE YOU GONNA FREEZE OR TAKE FLIGHT?
>OR ARE YOU MAN ENOUGH TO FIGHT?
>
>WHOA AY OH OH OH OOH OH
>WHOA AY OH OH OH OOH OH
>WHOA AY OH OH OH OOH OH
>WHOA AY OH OH OH OOH OH

(**TOBY** *goes and finds* **ANDREW**.)

TOBY.
>THIS KID IS NOT MESSING AROUND,
>HE NEARLY BIT MY EAR OFF.

ANDREW. What?!

TOBY.
>HE'S A BLACK BELT OF THE HIGHEST RANKS.

ANDREW.
>UM...
>NOPE.
>NEVERMIND,
>NO THANKS.

TOBY.
>IT'S TOO LATE NOW,
>HE'S COMING SOON
>TO HAVE HIS DEADLY WAY WITH YOU.
>I TRIED TO TALK HIM DOWN,
>BUT HE THREW ME TO THE GROUND.

ANDREW.

I DON'T STAND A CHANCE!
I DON'T WANNA DIE!

TOBY.

C'MON AND PUT ON YOUR BIG BOY PANTS
AND DECIDE.

TOBY & ILLYRIANS.

WHAT KIND OF MAN ARE YOU GONNA BE?
WHAT KIND OF MAN ARE YOU GONNA BE?
ARE YOU GONNA RUN, RUN AWAY.
OR ARE YOU GONNA SAVE THE DAY?
WHAT KIND OF MAN ARE YOU GONNA BE?
WHAT KIND OF MAN ARE YOU GONNA BE?
ARE YOU GONNA FREEZE OR TAKE FLIGHT?
OR ARE YOU MAN ENOUGH TO FIGHT?

WHOA AY OH OH OH OOH OH
WHOA AY OH OH OH OOH OH
WHOA AY OH OH OH OOH OH
WHOA AY OH OH OH OOH OH

(A training montage!)

*(**ANDREW** and **VIOLA** retreat to their corners and are given water/towels as they soliloquize.)*

VIOLA.

WHAT KIND OF MAN AM I GONNA BE?
IF I FIGHT HIM, THEY'LL FIND OUT
I'M NO KIND OF MAN TODAY
BUT IF I DON'T THEY'LL THINK
I'M NOT MUCH OF A MAN ANYWAY.
MY BROTHER IS THE ONE WHO CAN THROW A PUNCH.
I WAS THE WIMPY KID WHO SAT ALONE AT LUNCH.
BUT HEY, IF THESE PANTS HAVE MADE ME A LOVER
MAYBE THESE GLOVES CAN MAKE ME A FIGHTER.

VIOLA.

THEY ALL THINK I'M MAN ENOUGH TO FIGHT.

ANDREW.

STAY CALM, STAY CALM.

VIOLA.

OH, DISGUISE.

ANDREW.

I MISS MY MOM.

VIOLA.

COULD THEY BE RIGHT?

ANDREW.

I'M NOT THIS TYPE OF KNIGHT!

ANDREW & VIOLA.

WHAT KIND OF MAN AM I?
WHAT KIND OF MAN IS HE?
WHAT KIND OF MAN AM I SUPPOSED TO BE?

> (**TOBY** *becomes the referee in the ring as the* **ILLYRIANS** *cheer on the impending fight.* **ANDREW** *and* **VIOLA** *slowly approach each other, swords tentatively drawn.*)

TOBY.

MOMENT OF TRUTH, MY MEN.

ILLYRIANS.

MOMENT OF TRUTH, MY MEN.

TOBY.

PUSH HAS COME TO SHOVE.

ILLYRIANS.

PUSH HAS COME TO SHOVE.

TOBY.

SAY A PRAYER,

TOBY & ILLYRIANS.
> HOLD UP YOUR GLOVE,
> NOWHERE TO RUN,
> SO TELL ME, SON.
> WHAT KIND OF MAN ARE YOU GONNA BE?

VIOLA & ANDREW.
> I'M GONNA BE

TOBY & ILLYRIANS.
> WHAT KIND OF MAN ARE YOU GONNA BE?

VIOLA & ANDREW.
> I'M GONNA BE

TOBY & ILLYRIANS.
> WHAT KIND OF MAN ARE YOU GONNA BE?
> GONNA BE? GONNA BE? GONNA BE? GONNA BE?

> *(Just as they are about to begin fighting each other, the song is abruptly cut off as **ANTONIO** rushes in, stepping in front of **VIOLA**, his sword drawn:)*

ANTONIO. Put up your sword! If this young gentleman Have done offense, I take the fault on me: If you offend him, I for him defy you.

TOBY. You, sir! Why, what are you?

ANTONIO. One, sir, that for his love dares yet do more Than you have heard him brag to you he will.

TOBY. Nay, if you be an undertaker, I am for you.

> *(They draw their swords. Two **OFFICERS** enter.)*

FABIAN. O good Sir Toby, hold! Here come officers.

TOBY. I'll be with you anon!

FIRST OFFICER. This is the man; do thy office.

SECOND OFFICER. Antonio, I arrest thee at the suit of Duke Orsino.

ANTONIO. You do mistake me, sir.

FIRST OFFICER. No, sir, no jot; I know your favor well. Take him away!

ANTONIO. I must obey.

(*To* **VIOLA**.*)* This comes with seeking you:
But there's no remedy; I shall answer it.

SECOND OFFICER. Come, sir, away.

ANTONIO. I must entreat of you some of that money I did give you.

VIOLA. What money, sir?
For the fair kindness you have showed me here,
I'll lend you something: my having is not much;
Hold, there's half my coffer.

ANTONIO. Will you deny me now?

SECOND OFFICER. Come, sir, I pray you, go.

ANTONIO. Let me speak a little. This youth that you see here I snatched one half out of the jaws of death, Relieved him with such sanctity of love!

FIRST OFFICER. What's that to us? The time goes by: away!

ANTONIO. But O how vile an idol proves this god!
Thou hast done good feature shame, Sebastian!

[MUSIC 14 – VIOLA'S SOLILOQUY (REPRISE)]

VIOLA. Sebastian?

FIRST OFFICER. The man grows mad.

SECOND OFFICER. Away with him!

(The **OFFICERS** *drag off* **ANTONIO.** *The* **ILLYRIANS** *file out, bummed and confused that they're not getting the duel they came to see.* **TOBY** *shakes his head at* **VIOLA.***)*

TOBY. A very dishonest boy, and more a coward than a hare. Come hither, Andrew. Fabian.

*(***TOBY** *exits with* **ANDREW** *and* **FABIAN.***)*

VIOLA.
HE CALLED ME SEBASTIAN.
SEBASTIAN,
ARE YOU STILL OUT THERE SOMEWHERE?
COULD THAT BE TRUE?

SEBASTIAN,
WHAT WOULD YOU DO?
WHO AM I BESIDES HALF OF YOU?

Scene Thirteen
Olivia's Courtyard

*(**VIOLA** exits just as **SEBASTIAN** is entering, missing each other by seconds yet again.)*

*(Some **ILLYRIANS** are hanging out by the busking musicians and they notice him, mistaking him for **VIOLA/CESARIO**.)*

ILLYRIAN #8. Hey Cesario!

SEBASTIAN. Huh?

FESTE. Countess Olivia is looking for you.

SEBASTIAN. I prithee, vent thy folly somewhere else. Thou know'st not me.

FESTE. Vent my folly? I prithee now, ungird thy strangeness and tell me what I shall vent to Olivia. Shall I vent to her that thou art coming?

SEBASTIAN. I prithee, foolish Greek, depart from me. There's money for thee.

(He puts a coin in Feste's tip jar.)

FESTE. Well held out! No, I do not know you, nor your name is not Cesario, nor this is not my nose either. It's opposite day!

*(**FESTE** heads back to her piano as **TOBY** and **ANDREW** enter.)*

ANDREW. Now, sir, have I met you again? There's for you.

*(**ANDREW** punches **SEBASTIAN**, and **SEBASTIAN** punches him right back.)*

SEBASTIAN. Why, there's for thee, and there, and there. Are all the people mad?!

TOBY. Hold, sir!

(**TOBY** *grabs* **SEBASTIAN.**)

SEBASTIAN. Let go thy hand!

TOBY. Come, sir, I will not let you go. You are well fleshed.

(**SEBASTIAN** *pulls free and draws his sword.*)

SEBASTIAN. What wouldst thou now?

TOBY. What, what?

(**TOBY** *draws his sword.* **OLIVIA** *enters, accompanied by the* **HORN TRIO.**)

[MUSIC 14a – OLIVIA'S FANFARE #5]

OLIVIA. Hold, Toby! On thy life I charge thee, hold!

TOBY. Madam!

OLIVIA. Ungracious wretch, out of my sight!

(**TOBY** *and* **ANDREW** *exit.*)

Be not offended, dear Cesario. I prithee, gentle friend,
go with me to my house. Do not deny.

SEBASTIAN. Or I am mad, or else this is a dream:
If it be thus to dream, still let me sleep!

OLIVIA. Nay, come, I prithee!

SEBASTIAN. Madam, I will!

(**OLIVIA** *and* **SEBASTIAN** *exit.*)

Scene Fourteen
In the Port-A-Potty

*(**MALVOLIO** has been locked inside a Port-A-Potty toilet by **TOBY** as a prank – this is the "dark room" **TOBY** mentioned earlier. The door is covered in duct tape so he can't get out. **TOBY** and **MARIA** stand outside of it, taunting him. The band plays:)*

[MUSIC 14b – PORT-A-POTTY ENTRANCE]

MALVOLIO. Hello? Hello?

TOBY. *(Disguising his voice.)* What ho, I say! Peace in this prison!

MALVOLIO. Who calls there?

TOBY. *(Disguising his voice.)* Sir Topas, the priest, who comes to visit Malvolio the lunatic!

MARIA. *(Whispering to **TOBY**.)* My most exquisite Sir Topas!

MALVOLIO. Sir Topas, never was man thus wronged. Good Sir Topas, do not think I am mad. They have laid me here in hideous darkness!

TOBY. *(Disguising his voice.)* Out, hyperbolical fiend! Remain thou still in darkness!

MALVOLIO. Sir Topas???

TOBY. *(Back in his own voice, to **MARIA**.)* I would we were well rid of this knavery. If Malvolio may be conveniently delivered, I would he were, for I am now so far in offense with my niece that I cannot pursue with any safety this sport to the upshot. Feste, go to him in thine own voice, and bring me word how thou findest him.

FESTE. Me? No!

TOBY. Come by and by to my chamber.

> *(**TOBY** and **MARIA** exit.)*

> *(**MALVOLIO** recognizes **FESTE**'s voice.)*

MALVOLIO. Fool? Fool?

> *(**FESTE** tries to sneak away.)*

Good fool, I say?

> *(**FESTE** sighs and approaches the Port-A-Potty.)*

FESTE. Malvolio?

MALVOLIO. Ay, good fool, help me to some light.

FESTE. Do you remember what you said?

"Madam, why laugh you at such a barren rascal!"

MALVOLIO. Good fool!

FESTE. Tell me true, are you not mad indeed?

[MUSIC 15 – GREATNESS]

MALVOLIO.
I HATE THE DARK.
I'M NOT CRAZY.
IS THAT A BAT?!

> *(He shoos away what he thinks was a bat – then waits a moment to see if it returns.)*

AM I CRAZY?

I DID EXACTLY WHAT SHE SAID TO DO.
I SHOULD'VE KNOWN THIS WAS TOO GOOD TO BE TRUE.
IS THIS WHAT I GET FOR DOING EV'RYTHING RIGHT?
IS THIS MY DUE?

MALVOLIO.

> IF SOME ARE BORN GREAT,
> AND SOME ACHIEVE GREATNESS,
> AND SOME HAVE GREATNESS THRUST UPON THEM,
> THEN I CAN'T HELP THAT I WAS BORN GREAT!
> I DIDN'T ASK TO BE THE BEST.
> THINGS WOULD BE MUCH EASIER
> BEING AV'RAGE LIKE THE REST.
>
> NO ONE'S EVER UNDERSTOOD ME.
> IT'S NOTHING REALLY NEW.
> IN MIDDLE SCHOOL THEY LOCKED ME IN A LOCKER,
> ALWAYS PICKED ME LAST IN GYM CLASS SOCCER.
> I THINK EV'RYONE WAS SCARED BECAUSE
> OF HOW VIRTUOUS AND SMART I WAS,
> 'CAUSE MY MOM SAID:
> "DON'T LET THE BULLIES GET YOU DOWN, MALVOLIO.
> YOU ARE A VERY SPECIAL BOY, MALVOLIO.
> AND SOMEDAY THEY'LL ALL SEE."
> SO WHY HAS NO ONE REALIZED MY GREATNESS BUT ME?
>
> THEY SAY I'M SNOBBY,
> BUT I JUST HAVE HIGH STANDARDS
> FOR MY PRECIOUS TIME.
> IS THAT A CRIME?
>
> THEY SAY I'M POWER HUNGRY,
> BUT I'M JUST REACHING FOR THE STARS
> WHERE I BELONG.
> IS THAT SO WRONG?
>
> THEY SAY I'M VAIN,
> BUT LOVING YOURSELF IS A HEALTHY THING!
> THEY SAY I'M STRICT,
> BUT SOMEONE'S GOT TO KEEP THINGS RUNNING!
>
> I'M CRAZY, SO THEY SAY.
> WELL, CALL ME CRAZY,

BUT IF BEING ME IS CRAZY,
THEN LET THEM LAUGH AWAY!

YES, I WAS BORN GREAT,
AND I WILL ACHIEVE GREATNESS,
AND I WON'T BE AFRAID OF MY OWN FATE.
I'LL WRITE THEM ALL A LETTER
SAYING I DESERVE MUCH BETTER
AND MOM, I'LL MAKE YOU PROUD, JUST YOU WAIT.

SOMETIMES IT'S LONELY BEING GREAT.

FESTE. I will fetch you light.

MALVOLIO. I will live to be thankful to thee.

Scene Fifteen
Olivia's Balcony

(**SEBASTIAN** *enters in a daze on Olivia's balcony outside her bedchamber.*)

[MUSIC 16 – SEBASTIAN'S SOLILOQUY]

SEBASTIAN.
MY SISTER IS THE ONE WHO KNOWS WHAT TO DO
WHAT WOULD SHE CHOOSE IN MY UNTIED SHOES?
PLAY ALONG OR TRY AND SUSS OUT WHAT WENT WRONG?
THE LADY THINKS I'M SOMEONE ELSE
BUT SHE MAKES ME FEEL MORE LIKE MYSELF
SO...
I'M NOT SURE!
WHO AM I BESIDES HOW I LOOK TO HER?

(**OLIVIA** *enters and joins* **SEBASTIAN** *[no horn trio with her, as she is inside her house].*)

OH, OH OLIVIA!

(*Music continues under the following:*)

OLIVIA. Blame not this haste of mine. If you mean well, Now here, before this holy woman

(*An* **ILLYRIAN OFFICIANT** *enters.*)

Plight me the full assurance of your faith; that my most jealous and too doubtful soul may live at peace. What do you say?

SEBASTIAN. I'll follow this good lady, and go with you; and, having sworn truth, ever will be true.

ILLYRIAN OFFICIANT. By the power vested in me by the state of Illyria, I now pronounce you, Cesario and Olivia, husband and wife! You may kiss the groom!

OLIVIA & SEBASTIAN.
WE ARE NOW BELOVED!

Scene Sixteen
Finale in the Town Square

(The **ILLYRIANS** *enter to see what the heck all the commotion is about.)*

[MUSIC 17 – WORD ON THE STREET III]

ILLYRIANS.
> DID YOU HEAR THE WORD, WORD, WORD
> ON THE STREET?
> DID YOU HEAR THE WORD, WORD, WORD
> ON THE STREET?

ILLYRIAN #1.
> THERE'S BEEN SOME TOP SECRET NUPTIALS,
> DID YOU KNOW?

ILLYRIAN #5.
> IS IT THE DUKE?

ILLYRIAN #3.
> THE COUNTESS?

ILLYRIANS.
> WHO?!

ILLYRIAN #1.
> OLIVIA ELOPED WITH CESARIO.

ILLYRIAN #7.
> AN ELOPEMENT!

ILLYRIAN #6.
> I CAN'T BELIEVE THEY ROBBED US OF A ROYAL WEDDING!

ILLYRIAN #8.
> SO ROMANTIC, THOUGH!

ILLYRIAN #4.
> DOES ORSINO KNOW
> 'BOUT THE NEW "IT" COUPLE OF ILLYRIA?

ILLYRIAN #5.

    CESARIOLIVIA!!

ILLYRIANS.

    IF MUSIC BE THE FOOD OF LOVE, PLAY ON!

    IF MUSIC BE THE FOOD OF LOVE, PLAY ON!

    IF MUSIC BE THE FOOD OF LOVE, PLAY ON!

    PLAY ON!

    PLAY ON!

       (**VIOLA** *and* **ORSINO** *enter.*)

       (*The* **OFFICERS** *bring on* **ANTONIO***, in handcuffs.*)

FIRST OFFICER. Make way!

VIOLA. Here comes the man, sir, that did rescue me.

ORSINO. That face of his I do remember well.

FIRST OFFICER. Here in the streets, desperate of shame and state,

    In private brabble did we apprehend him.

VIOLA. He did me kindness, sir, drew on my side;

    But in conclusion put strange speech upon me.

    I know not what 'twas but distraction.

ORSINO. Thou salt-water thief!

    What foolish boldness brought thee to their mercies,

    Whom thou, in terms so bloody and so dear,

    Hast made thine enemies?

ANTONIO. Orsino, noble sir,

    A witchcraft drew me hither:

    That most ingrateful boy there by your side,

    From the rude sea's enraged and foamy mouth

    Did I redeem. For his sake

    Did I expose myself, pure for his love,

    Into the danger of this adverse town.

VIOLA. How can this be?

ORSINO. When came he to this town?

ANTONIO. Today, my lord; and for three months before,
Both day and night did we keep company.

[MUSIC 17a – OLIVIA'S FANFARE #6]

ORSINO. Here comes the countess: now heaven walks on
earth. But for thee, fellow; thy words are madness:
Three months this youth hath tended upon me;
But more of that anon. Take him aside.

> (**OLIVIA** *enters.*)

OLIVIA. (*Cutting off the* **HORN TRIO**, *finally fed up with
them.*) Oh enough already!

> (*The* **HORN TRIO** *stops playing, shrugs, and
> re-joins the bandstand.*)

Cesario, you do not keep promise with me.

VIOLA. Madam?

ORSINO. Gracious Olivia –

OLIVIA. What do you say, Cesario?

VIOLA. My lord would speak; my duty hushes me.

OLIVIA. If it be aught to the old tune, my lord,
It is as fat and fulsome to mine ear
As howling after music.

ORSINO. Still so cruel?

OLIVIA. Still so constant, lord.

ORSINO. This your minion, whom I know you love,
And whom, by heaven I swear, I tender dearly,
Him will I tear out of that cruel eye,
Where he sits crowned in his master's spite.

ORSINO. Come, boy, with me; my thoughts are ripe in mischief:

I'll sacrifice the lamb that I do love,

To spite a raven's heart within a dove.

VIOLA. And I, most apt and willingly,

To do you rest, a thousand deaths would die.

OLIVIA. Where goes Cesario?

VIOLA. After him I love

More than I love these eyes, more than my life,

More, by all mores, than e'er I shall love wife.

OLIVIA. Ay me, detested! How am I beguiled!

VIOLA. Who does beguile you? Who does do you wrong?

OLIVIA. Hast thou forgot thyself? Is it so long?

Call forth the holy mother.

(**MARIA** *exits to go get the* **OFFICIANT**.)

ORSINO. *(To* **VIOLA**.*)* Come, away!

OLIVIA. Whither, my lord? Cesario, husband, stay.

ORSINO. Husband!

OLIVIA. Ay, husband: can he that deny?

ORSINO. Her husband, boy?

VIOLA. No, my lord, not I.

(**MARIA** *leads the* **ILLYRIAN OFFICIANT** *on.*)

OLIVIA. Fear not, Cesario. Mother, I charge thee, by thy reverence, here to unfold, what hath newly passed between this youth and me.

ILLYRIAN OFFICIANT. A contract of eternal bond of love, confirmed by interchangement of your rings.

ORSINO. *(To* **VIOLA**.*)* O thou dissembling cub!

VIOLA. My lord, I do protest –

(**ANDREW** *enters, in pain.*)

ANDREW. For the love of God, a surgeon! He has broke my head across! For the love of God, your help!

OLIVIA. Who has done this, Sir Andrew?

ANDREW. Cesario! We took him for a coward, but he's the very devil incardinate.

ORSINO. My gentleman, Cesario?

ANDREW. Here he is! You broke my head for nothing!

VIOLA. Why do you speak to me? I never hurt you.

(**TOBY** *enters limping and* **MARIA** *rushes to help him.*)

ANDREW. Here comes Sir Toby. You shall hear more!

ORSINO. How now, gentleman! How is't with you?

TOBY. That's all one: has hurt me, and there's the end on't.

(*To* **FESTE.**) Sot, didst see Dick Surgeon, sot?

FESTE. Oh, he's drunk.

OLIVIA. Who hath made this havoc with them?

[MUSIC 18 – VIOLA'S SOLILOQUY (2ND REPRISE)]

(**SEBASTIAN** *enters and approaches* **OLIVIA.** *He does not yet notice* **VIOLA.**)

SEBASTIAN. I am sorry, sweet one, I have hurt your kinsman,
But, had it been the brother of my blood,
I must have done no less with wit and safety.
You throw a strange regard upon me, and by that
I do perceive it hath offended you.

ORSINO. One face, one voice, one habit, and two persons!

ANTONIO. Sebastian?

SEBASTIAN. O my dear Antonio!

ANTONIO. How have you made division of yourself?
An apple, cleft in two, is not more twin
Than these two creatures. Which is Sebastian?

(SEBASTIAN finally turns and sees VIOLA.)

VIOLA.
SEBASTIAN?

SEBASTIAN.
MY EYES ARE PLAYING TRICKS ON ME.

VIOLA.
IS IT REALLY YOU?

SEBASTIAN.
IT CAN'T BE TRUE.
YOU DROWNED, OR DID I?
IS THIS WHERE YOU GO WHEN YOU DIE?

VIOLA.
SEBASTIAN, IT'S ME.
VIOLA.

ORSINO & OLIVIA. Viola?

VIOLA.
OUR MOTHER HAD A BIRTHMARK ON HER SHOULDER,
AND OUR DAD DIED WHEN WE WERE THIRTEEN.
WE GREW UP IN A HOUSE BY THE BAY IN MESSALINE.

SEBASTIAN.
VIOLA!

(VIOLA and SEBASTIAN embrace.)

SEBASTIAN & VIOLA.
I NEVER THOUGHT THIS WOULD BE

SEBASTIAN.

WAIT, WHY ARE YOU DRESSED LIKE ME?

VIOLA.

I THOUGHT I'D LOST YOU, AND I WAS LOST TOO.
SO I WORE YOUR SHOES
AND THEY MADE ME STRONG.
BUT NOW THAT YOU'RE FOUND,
I THINK I'VE BEEN HERE ALL ALONG, BECAUSE
MAYBE THE MAN I TRIED TO BE IS THE GIRL I ALWAYS WAS.

(**VIOLA** *takes off her hat, or some other part of
her disguise, and holds it in her hand.*)

SO DISGUISE, YOU WERE THE DEVIL'S BLESSING.
YOU TURNED A MIRROR BACK AT ME
AND FOR THE FIRST TIME, I THINK I LIKE WHAT I SEE.
NOW I CAN PUT YOU BACK ON THE SHELF
AND CHANGE INTO MYSELF.

ORSINO. *(To* **VIOLA.***)* Cesario?

VIOLA. Viola.

ORSINO. Viola.

[MUSIC 19 – TELL HER (REPRISE)]

Thou hast said to me a thousand times
Thou never shouldst love woman like to me.

VIOLA. And all those sayings will I over-swear.

ORSINO.

I CAN'T BELIEVE HOW BLIND I'VE BEEN,
STEWING IN MY SAD OLD SONG.
SORRY OLIVIA,
I PUT MY LOVE WHERE IT DID NOT BELONG
WHEN ALL THIS TIME MY MELODY
WAS SINGING RIGHT IN FRONT OF ME.

ORSINO.
I WANT YOU,
I HOPE YOU
WILL LET ME BE YOUR MAN.
NOW I UNDERSTAND.
I WANT YOU,

VIOLA.
I WANT YOU,

VIOLA & ORSINO.
I NEED YOU.

(**VIOLA** *gets down on one knee.*)

VIOLA.
SO TELL ME IF YOU MIGHT
MARRY ME TONIGHT?

ORSINO. Here is my hand!

(**VIOLA** *and* **ORSINO** *kiss as everybody cheers!*)

[MUSIC 20 – I AM SHE (REPRISE)]

OLIVIA. Most wonderful!

SEBASTIAN. Olivia, so comes it, you have been mistook. But nature to her bias drew in that.

(**OLIVIA** *takes* **SEBASTIAN**'s *hand.*)

OLIVIA.
SEBASTIAN,
NOW I SEE YOU FOR WHO YOU REALLY ARE.
YOU'RE LOVELY
AND FREE
SO HEY, IT WORKS FOR ME.

(**OLIVIA** *turns to* **VIOLA.**)

AND AS FOR YOU
I HEREBY DECREE

YOU ARE MY SISTER.
YOU ARE SHE.

OLIVIA & VIOLA.
YOU ARE MY SISTER.
YOU ARE SHE.

OLIVIA. *(To* **ORSINO.***)* My lord, so please you, to think me as well a sister.

ORSINO. *(To* **OLIVIA.***)* Madam, I am most apt to embrace your offer.

OLIVIA. *(To* **MARIA.***)* Maria, fetch Malvolio hither.
And yet, alas, now I remember me,
They say, poor gentleman, he's much distract.
Bring him hither.

> *(***MARIA** *enlists some* **ILLYRIANS** *to help her roll on the Port-A-Potty. They try in vain to unlock the taped-up door and the Port-A-Potty falls over.* **MALVOLIO** *comes tumbling out, kicking the door open. Everyone holds their noses at the stench.)*

MALVOLIO. Madam, you have done me wrong, notorious wrong!

OLIVIA. Have I, Malvolio? No.

MALVOLIO. Lady, you have. Pray you, peruse this letter.
You must not now deny it is your hand!

> *(***MALVOLIO** *hands her the letter and she reads.)*

OLIVIA. Alas, Malvolio, this is not my writing,
Though, I confess, much like the character.
But out of question 'tis Maria's hand.

(All eyes turn toward **MARIA** *who sheepishly comes forward.)*

MARIA. Good madam, hear me speak,
Most freely I confess, myself and Toby
Set this device against Malvolio here.
I writ the letter at Sir Toby's great importance
In recompense whereof...

(She flashes a big ring.)

TOBY. I hath married her!

MARIA. He hath married me!

TOBY. How with a sportful malice it was followed,
May rather pluck on laughter than revenge.

OLIVIA. Alas, poor Malvolio, how have they baffled thee!

FESTE. And thus the whirligig of time brings in his revenges.

[MUSIC 21 – MALVOLIO'S EXIT]

MALVOLIO.
I WAS BORN GREAT
AND I WILL ACHIEVE GREATNESS
AND I'LL THRUST MY GREATNESS ALL OVER YOUR FACES.
I'VE LET YOU WIN FOR FAR TOO LONG.
SO WATCH OUT, I'M GONNA PROVE YOU BULLIES WRONG!

AND BEFORE I AM THROUGH,
I'LL GET EVEN WITH YOU.
YES, YOU'RE GONNA GET
– THE WHOLE PACK OF YOU –
YOU'RE ALL GONNA GET
– AND YOU AND YOU! –
YOUR DUE!

I hope you're all very happy together.

> (**MALVOLIO** *exits with much fanfare.*)

VIOLA. *(To the* **ILLYRIAN OFFICIANT**.*)* I pray you, madam, marry us!

> (**ORSINO** *and* **VIOLA** *are married under the following. All the* **ILLYRIANS** *participate as the* **ILLYRIAN OFFICIANT** *sings, leading the ceremony.*)

[MUSIC 22 – IS THIS NOT LOVE? (REPRISE)]

ILLYRIAN OFFICIANT.
IS THIS NOT LOVE?
IS THIS NOT LOVE THAT I FEEL FOR YOU?
DO YOU FEEL IT TOO?
IS THIS NOT LOVE?
IS THIS NOT LOVE?

COUPLES & ALL.
IS THIS NOT LOVE?
IS THIS NOT LOVE THAT I FEEL FOR YOU?
DO YOU FEEL IT TOO?
IS THIS NOT LOVE?
IS THIS NOT LOVE?
LOVE! LOVE!
LOVE! LOVE!

> (**VIOLA** *and* **ORSINO** *kiss – they are now married!*)

> (*The ceremony turns into a raucous reception in the town square.*)

> (*The* **ILLYRIANS** *celebrate with a big community wedding dance party.*)

[MUSIC 23 – EYES OF ANOTHER]

OLIVIA & ORSINO.
> OH, I USED TO THINK I COULD
> I COULD READ YOU LIKE A STORYBOOK.
> JUST BECAUSE OF HOW YOU LOOK.

VIOLA & SEBASTIAN.
> BUT AFTER WALKING IN YOUR BOOTS
> I CAN'T BELIEVE HOW WRONG I WAS.
> I'LL NEVER THINK THE SAME BECAUSE,

VIOLA.
> BROTHER,

ALL.
> I HAD NO CLUE, I HAD NO CLUE WHAT YOU GO THROUGH.
> I JUST ASSUMED, BUT I ASSUMED
> THINGS THAT AIN'T TRUE
> BUT I FEEL WHERE YOU'RE COMING FROM
> 'CAUSE NOW I'VE BEEN THERE TOO,
> AND I SEE THROUGH THE EYES OF ANOTHER

FESTE.
> EYES OF ANOTHER

ALL.
> HEAR THROUGH THE EARS OF SOMEBODY ELSE.
> IF WE'D OPEN OUR HEARTS TO EACH OTHER'S BEAT,
> WHAT A BETTER WORLD IT COULD BE.
> WHAT A BETTER
> WHAT, WHAT A BETTER
> WHAT A BETTER
> WHAT, WHAT A BETTER
> WHAT A BETTER
> WHAT, WHAT

>   (**MALVOLIO** *is dragged back onstage by a group of kids, and despite himself, gets swept up in the song.*)

MALVOLIO.

A BETTER WORLD IT COULD BE.

ALL.

LET'S TRADE PLACES FOR A DAY.
YOU BE ME AND I'LL BE YOU
YOU WALK MY STREET,
I'LL WEAR YOUR SHOES.
MEET ME HERE WHEN DAY IS DONE.
WE'LL SWITCH BACK TO OUR OWN SKIN
AND TELL EACH OTHER WHERE WE'VE BEEN,
SAYIN'
I HAD NO CLUE, I HAD NO CLUE
WHAT YOU GO THROUGH.
I JUST ASSUMED, BUT I ASSUMED
THINGS THAT AIN'T TRUE

> (**ORSINO** *removes* **ANTONIO**'s *handcuffs, pardoning him.*)

ORSINO.

SO REMIND ME TO BE KINDER,
'CAUSE NOW I'VE BEEN THERE, TOO.

ALL.

AND I SEE THROUGH THE EYES OF ANOTHER.

ANTONIO.

EYES OF ANOTHER!

> (**ANDREW** *begins to dance with* **ILLYRIAN #5**, *at the encouragement of* **TOBY**.)

ALL.

HEAR THROUGH THE EARS OF SOMEBODY ELSE.
IF WE'D OPEN OUR HEARTS TO EACH OTHER'S BEAT,
WHAT A BETTER WORLD IT COULD BE.

> (**MALVOLIO** *catches* **ANTONIO**'s *eye and they meet-cute. They start to dance together.*)

ALL.

WHAT A BETTER, WHAT WHAT A BETTER
WHAT A BETTER, WHAT WHAT A BETTER
WHAT A BETTER, WHAT WHAT
A BETTER WORLD IT COULD BE.

(Dance break!)

IF WE'D SEE THROUGH THE EYES OF ANOTHER.

FESTE.

EYES OF ANOTHER

ALL.

HEAR THROUGH THE EARS OF SOMEBODY ELSE.
IF WE'D OPEN OUR HEARTS TO EACH OTHER'S BEAT,
WHAT A BETTER WORLD IT COULD BE.

FESTE.

IF WE'D ONLY

ALL.

SEE THROUGH THE EYES OF ANOTHER.

FESTE.

EYES OF ANOTHER,

ALL.

HEAR THROUGH THE EARS OF SOMEBODY ELSE.
IF WE'D OPEN OUR HEARTS TO EACH OTHER'S BEAT,
WHAT A BETTER WORLD IT COULD BE.
WHAT A BETTER WORLD IT COULD BE.

End of Play

[MUSIC 24 – BOWS]